I0664616

A Little Night Murder

J.S. Cook

Dreamspinner Press

Published by
Dreamspinner Press
5032 Capital Circle SW
Suite 2, PMB# 279
Tallahassee, FL 32305-7886
USA
http://www.dreamspinnerpress.com/

A Little Night Murder
© 2013 J.S. Cook.

Cover Art
© 2013 Catt Ford.
Cover content is for illustrative purposes only and any person depicted on the cover is a model.

ISBN: 978-1-62798-160-6
Digital ISBN: 978-1-62798-161-3

Printed in the United States of America
First Edition
September 2013

To Lola and the Big Guy. You make everything so much better.

Chapter One

September, 1942
New York

I SHOULD have never opened that door. At least that's what I keep telling myself. Of course, it didn't really matter if I opened it or not: five'll get you ten that Nicky's boys would have ignored the door and shot me right through it. That's the kind of boys they are. That's the kind of boy Nicky is—or was—and I had no excuse. I knew this was going to happen to me, sooner or later.

For my own safety and because he insisted, I'd been staying at Sam Lipinski's apartment on Findlay Avenue in the Bronx. It was late September, but the city seemed to be hanging on to summer, and the days were long and lush and golden, with cool nights just perfect for sleeping, if that was what you wanted to do at night. I'd been staying there a couple of days and nothing bad had happened, or at least, nothing much. I knew better than to expect it'd stay that way, especially with what I had hanging over my head. It was inevitable that things were going to catch up with me, and unless I suddenly manifested the ability to disappear into thin air, Nicky Brooks's boys would be around to pay a visit.

About four o'clock in the afternoon, maybe a little after, I heard a knock on the door, a polite rapping sound like somebody makes when they think you're not home. I wasn't sure if I should answer it, so I waited, but I guess my curiosity got the better of me. It usually does. I wasn't completely stupid, so I peered through the fish-eye that looked out into the corridor.

Sam had warned me some of the neighbor kids liked ringing doorbells and running away, and sometimes they left a little gift behind, rotten eggs or somebody else's putrid garbage. Mrs. Neumann, an old lady from two floors up, liked banging on doors in the middle of the afternoon so she could come in and talk your ear off, and sometimes the super liked to snoop around on the pretext of checking the plumbing or some other excuse.

Do they know you're a cop? I'd asked Sam. I was willing to wager they knew when he went to bed and when he got up, what he ate for breakfast, and what color underwear he was wearing any given morning.

Of course they do, Sam said. *Why do you think they're so goddamn nosy?*

THE man at the door was maybe five and a half feet tall, with bright-red hair escaping from underneath his Western Union cap and a spray of freckles across his nose. "Sam Lipinski?"

"No. I can take the telegram for him, though."

At first glance he looked like any other messenger boy, until you saw his eyes. Cold, opaque, and empty. The eyes of a professional killer. "This message is all for you, Frankie-Boy. Nobody but you. Special delivery from Nicky Brooks." He drew an automatic from somewhere inside his coat and squeezed the trigger; the slugs crashed into me at point-blank range, leaving behind a trail of burning agony. I felt hot and weak and sick, and my legs couldn't hold me up anymore. Then a lot of doors opened, and a lot of people spilled out into the corridor. I heard someone shouting to call the police, call an ambulance, and somebody screamed. I kept telling myself to *get up, get up already* but nothing happened.

A young woman lifted my head into her lap; she said her name was Claire and she would stay with me. "Mrs. Neumann's gone to telephone an ambulance. You're going to be all right." I knew I wasn't going to be all right, but I didn't have the strength to explain it to her. Everything around me looked weird, small and far away, and I could taste blood at the back of my throat. The hallway seemed to stretch out to an impossible distance, then suddenly collapsed back again with the kind of rushing noise the wind makes in the subway. I figured maybe I was going to die, and that was just too bad.

I WAS in a white room. There was a whirring noise close by, and the sunlight coming through the blinds was hurting my eyes. I tried to sit up, but someone had driven three enormous staples through my gut directly into the bed, pinning me like some exotic insect. My hands lay on my chest, quiescent and still.

I was alive.

Police Lieutenant Sam Lipinski was sitting in the chair next to my bed, his head resting back against the wall, his mouth slightly open, and his breathing slow and even. He was rumpled, as if he'd slept in his clothes, and unshaven, and his tie had been yanked down. His black eyelashes made dark shadows on the paler skin under his eyes, and there were lines of fatigue on his face. He was sound asleep. I watched the slow flutter of his eyelids as he dreamed, his hands twitching, his breath catching in his throat. He looked gentler when he slept, less perennially watchful, as if the part of him that observed and waited was somewhere else. I liked looking at him; Sam is a handsome man.

He blinked, sat up, and looked at me, wide awake. "How are you feeling?"

"I'm alive," I said, "if not in one piece. Did the doc save me any souvenirs?" I'd never been shot before, and I wanted to keep at least one of the slugs Nicky's boy had put in me, for posterity. I thought about keeping it in a glass jar in my bathroom medicine

7

cabinet, somewhere close by, so I could remember. Or maybe I'd get it strung on a chain so I could wear it around my neck, some kind of lucky charm.

"Hurts?" He was trying not to grin, but I knew him. Sam and I had grown up in the same neighborhood.

"Like somebody dug my guts out with a rusty spoon." It was an apt simile, but I wasn't looking forward to how I'd feel once the drugs wore off. "But I'll live."

"Doc says it was close." Sam's dark eyes held my gaze. "Goddammit, what'd I tell you about opening the door?" Sam had been putting me up at his place until we could figure out what to do with me. Nicky Brooks was out of jail, and word on the street was he'd be gunning for me. Sam figured there was nowhere safer than a cop's apartment. He was wrong.

"I know, I know." It was just like Nicky to send a murderer dressed up as a telegraph boy. I knew him well enough to expect such things, and Sam was right: I should have never opened the door. "I'm sorry."

"I oughta slug you, that's what I oughta do, and I would, only you've been through hell." He raised one dark eyebrow. "You recognize the guy?"

"No, I'd never seen him before. Probably hired especially for the occasion. Nicky wouldn't bother sending one of his usual guys. He knows I'd recognize anybody he sent."

Sam's gaze flickered over my bandages. "They get all the slugs out?" I asked.

"Yeah. The doc said they did."

The last thing I remembered was a nurse pushing down on my abdomen while a young intern stuck his finger up my ass, checking for blood. Somebody yanked the pillows out from under my head and a black rubber mask was fitted over my face and I was gone, brother. Some people say you dream under anesthesia, but I never did. It was just a space of blackness sandwiched between two bouts of wakefulness and that was it.

"So tell me about him, this guy who shot you." Sam, ever the cop, reached into his inside pocket and pulled out a notebook. "What do you remember about him?"

"Red hair, kind of young, maybe twenty years old. Pimply face." It was hard to remember, hard to recall the details as they'd occurred. "He had an envelope—telegram—said it was for you. I told him I'd take it." Even now it had the surreal flavor of something that had happened to someone else.

"Yeah, you took it all right." He grimaced. "Anything else? Height, distinguishing marks, ethnicity?"

I shook my head, which was a big mistake. The room tilted and spun, and for a moment or two, I was sure I was going to vomit or pass out. "Sorry, Sam. I guess I'm not helping much, am I?"

"Anything you can give me is helping." He jotted down what I'd told him. "Did he say anything or do anything that seemed strange or unusual? Something that tipped you off?"

"He said the message was for me, from Nicky Brooks." My side twinged and I must have grunted, because Sam shut the notebook and stowed away the pen.

"You're tired. I'm gonna let you get some rest." He rose to go. "I've got a man on the door just in case Nicky tries again." Sam leaned over me. He was warm and he smelled really good, but then, he generally did. Sam is one of those guys who usually looks as crisp as a new dollar bill. "If you need anything, anything at all, you know where to find me."

I squeezed his hand. "I know. But Sam, you know he's going to try again. This is Nicky Brooks we're talking about. He's not gonna quit until he gets me—unless I get him first." Nicky Brooks, who'd already managed to cut a violent swath through my family, doing the kind of damage no amount of time will ever undo.

"Oh no you don't." His face settled into the same expression I'd seen him wear while interrogating hardened criminals. "Don't you even think about anything like that."

"Sam, it's me or him. You know that."

He stepped back from my bed, raised his arms in a gesture of futility, and let them fall. "Then you gotta concentrate on getting well so we can… I dunno, get you out of town or something. Maybe I can swing something—send you somewhere far away, someplace they ain't never heard of Nicky Brooks. I mean it, Frankie."

"That's a great idea, Sam, but where the hell am I gonna go? He found me at your place. He could probably find me anywhere. And what am I supposed to do? Sell apples on the street? In case you haven't noticed, there's a war on." So much for thinking we'd keep well out of it, but Pearl Harbor wasn't an insult you could easily overlook.

"Leave it with me," he said. "I'll figure something out, I promise. Frank, you need to rest. Rest, now. I'll be back tomorrow." He touched my arm. "If you hear or see anything that doesn't seem right, ring for the nurse. Don't wait."

I knew he was right, and dammit, I agreed with him, but I was suddenly tired, very tired, and my eyes were closing. Sleep was a deep, dark well, and I fell into it gladly.

Chapter Two

MY FIRST sight of Gander left me feeling pretty underwhelmed: a flat space of land in the middle of what looked to be endless bog, surrounded by low hills whose exposed bedrock had retained only the merest hint of anything resembling foliage. The short, stunted trees appeared to have been grasped by some invisible hand and violently twisted so they all faced the same direction. I had arrived.

As we taxied to a stop some distance from the terminal, I noticed dozens of curious, interested faces peering at us through a high, wire fence that had been erected around the airport's perimeter. I nudged my seating companion, a portly businessman type in a heavy overcoat who'd slept all the way from New York. "What's with the landing party?"

"Huh?" He peered past me out the window. "Oh, that. Airplanes are still a novelty around here. The locals don't get to see much." He heaved himself to his feet. "Don't look at 'em. And don't give 'em any money, that's my advice."

I followed him out and down onto the tarmac, walking quickly as a defense against the extremely brisk winds that threatened to tear open every last button on my coat. Inside, the terminal was bustling with uniforms, not the least of which were those of the RAF's Ferry Command, busily moving new aircraft to their final posting destinations in the European theater.

At the counter, I proffered my passport and waited while the clerk looked it and me over with a weather eye. "How come you're not overseas?" he asked. He was tall and thin, with an unfortunately beaky nose and black-rimmed glasses that kept slipping; I had no trouble imagining him standing on one leg in a bog, preening himself and catching flies.

"Bad lungs," I said, and coughed to make my point. "I had whooping cough as a kid."

"Huh." He sized me up like he didn't believe me. "From New York, aren't you?"

"Is that a crime?"

He raised his hands in mock self-defense. "Oh, it's no skin off my arse." He stamped my passport with more force than was strictly necessary and waved me toward a side door. "Baggage coming off in a few minutes. Welcome to Newfoundland."

I waited with the other bedraggled, flight-weary travelers beside the baggage claim area while my suitcase was shoved through a hole in the wall. There were several taxis lined up outside, so I picked the most likely one—almost expecting to see this guy I knew back in New York, Mark Donnelly—and told the driver, an antiquated specimen on the wrong side of fifty, to take me to the train station.

"'Merican, are ya?" He watched me in the rearview mirror, his toothless mouth furiously working a piece of chewing gum. "I can always tell the 'Mericans. Ye always got real nice clothes." He pronounced it *clowes*. "Where'd you get that coat you got on?"

"Uh, I don't remember." The cab bounced over a series of ruts in the road that sent me careening from one side of the car to the other. I clapped a hand on my head to keep my hat in place. "Hey, take it easy, will you?"

"Sorry, buddy. They been at the roads a lot lately. Trying to get it done before the snow comes. Awful lot of snow around here in the winter." He launched into an improbable tale involving himself, his grandfather, a horse, and a makeshift sled fashioned out of the front door of his grandmother's house. When I finally disembarked, I gave him a generous tip, mostly because I was thrilled not to have to listen to him anymore.

The train ride to St. John's was an uninspiring four hours through the same flat, forbidding terrain that gradually gave way to rolling hills and, finally, the sea. It reminded me of Maine in a lot of ways: there was the same grim coastline, the same winter bleakness about the landscape. If Hell was cold, it probably looked like this. By the time we slid into the station in St. John's, it was dark. I was rumpled and exhausted, and the dry turkey sandwich I'd had in the train's dining car seemed stuck in my throat. My first glimpse of the town was singularly uninspiring. Rows of rickety wooden houses were set at variance on either side of narrow, cobblestoned streets that reminded me of the slum district of Chicago.

Where in God's name had Sam sent me?

I went through to the street side of the station, looking in vain for a taxi to take me to my hotel, but at this late hour, there was nothing moving except a lone horse-drawn milk wagon clopping wearily up the street. I pulled out the hand-drawn map my new boss, Fred Koestler, had given me before I left New York. According to it, I was at the western extremity of Water Street, but my hotel was one street up and in the eastern part of town. Still suffering the aftereffect of having had three bullets taken out of my abdomen, I honestly couldn't contemplate walking that far carrying my heavy suitcase.

Koestler was the manager of Columbia All-Risk, a New York insurance firm setting up shop in Newfoundland. The war had shone a certain light on the island's strategic importance, and with the influx of British, American, and Canadian troops, the insurance boys were all set to make a killing—so to speak. They needed investigators, so Sam Lipinski figured it would fit the bill. He was a cop—who was I to argue?

Just then, there came an agitated tapping noise from the station behind me, and I turned to see one of the desk clerks motioning to me from the window. I went back inside. "Yes?"

"What are you standing out there like that for?" He was wearing a green visor like a blackjack dealer, antique sleeve garters, and ornate suspenders into which a repeating pattern of green, pink, and white had been laboriously worked. "Come in and I'll call Crotty's for ye."

"Crotty's?"

"The taxi, boy."

I waited while he shouted into the phone, and within moments, a heavy black car, its fenders painted with white blackout paint, pulled up to the curb. My first trip along Water Street—the town's main drag—was one of the most singular voyages I have ever taken. Because of the blackout, the entire street was as dark as the bottom of a well, with no light to be seen anywhere. The night was clear, however, and the full moon overhead allowed for a little illumination, so I was able to make out the low shapes of crouching buildings and the slow passage of streetcars down the middle of the road, their dark skins gleaming like the backs of huge, arcane beetles. The sight of brick buildings, the same kind I had been used to back home in the Bronx, reassured me. Maybe this wouldn't be so bad after all. Maybe both Fred Koestler and Sam were doing me a favor, and it was unlikely Nicky Brooks would come looking for me here.

The Newfoundland Hotel perched at the top of Duckworth Street was also minimally illuminated. A uniformed doorman greeted me and took my suitcase, ushering me inside. In contrast to the outside, the lobby was adequately lit and sumptuously decorated, and for the first time in a great many hours, I felt like I'd returned to civilization. I signed the register and followed the bellboy up to my room. The door opened on a pleasant scene: double bed, easy chair, desk—all the usual stuff. I tested the mattress with my hand; it seemed firm enough. Instead of the usual mint on the pillow, however, there was—

The bellhop, seeing my expression, must have thought I was off my nut. "Is everything all right, sir?"

I picked up the cufflink and held it out to him. "Did you lose something?"

"No, sir. We're issued official hotel cuff buttons, and we wear them whenever we're on duty." He examined it. "Are you sure it isn't yours, Mr. Boyle? Maybe it slipped out of your pocket by accident?"

It was gold, set with a ruby etched with the letter N. Yeah, I'd seen it before. I'd seen it in my nightmares. "It's not mine." I passed him some coin, advised him that would be all, and made sure to lock the door behind him. Everybody thinks a locked door makes you feel safe, but I knew there was nowhere safe for me in the entire world—nowhere I could go that Nicky Brooks wouldn't find me.

"I THINK you'll like this one." Fred Koestler pulled his dark, late-model sedan up in front of the stout stone tower that crowned the top of one of the windiest hills in the entire world. "If we don't blow to kingdom come first."

I followed him across the parking lot to a narrow walkway that led behind the tower. The sun was shining but the wind was absolutely eye-watering, and I reflexively hunched my head and shoulders in a self-protective posture. "Where are you taking me, Mr. Koestler?" Perhaps he was working for Nicky Brooks and his orders were to throw me off the hill.

"Just a little farther. This way."

We stood at the lip of an abyss made of jagged rock and hard water. A section of the cliff had been cordoned off with rope and signs were posted, warning trespassers away, but I didn't need to get close to figure out what had happened here. Two perfect footprints stood out in the frozen mud at the cliff's edge. There were no drag marks, no extra prints that would have indicated any kind of struggle or hesitation. The wide swath of winter-brown grass behind the tower tapered down to solid rock, then mud, which might have explained there being only two footprints, but I wasn't buying it.

Koestler turned to me. "Suicide?"

"Maybe. Only one set of prints. If it was murder, there'd be more." I turned it over in my mind. "If it was suicide, the prints would be from just one person, but there'd be a lot more of them. Nobody takes a flying leap off a cliff on the first try. They usually have to… rehearse it a little. Did the police find anything here?"

Koestler did something with his eyebrows. "Such as…?"

"Eyeglasses, pocketbook, handkerchief, cigarette lighter, shoes?"

He shook his head. "Not that I know of. The husband of the policyholder—her beneficiary—called us to report that his wife had killed herself by jumping off Signal Hill. The police never found her body. Not surprising, considering the elevation and the current below." He waved a hand at the water. "Go in there and you don't survive long enough to regret it. If the fall didn't kill her, the water temperature almost certainly did."

I was confused and told him so. "If she killed herself—I mean, if that's the foregone conclusion—then why do you need me? It sounds like the police have got this all tied up." A particularly vicious gust tore at the flaps of my overcoat and dragged icy fingers down my back. "Obviously the policy isn't payable—"

"Oh, but it is." Koestler took my arm and led me back toward the car. "That's just it, you see. The suicide clause only applies for the first two years of the policy." He held the car door for me, then got in on the other side. "So technically, they or their legal counsel can compel payment of the benefit." He turned the key, and the big car roared to life. "Mrs. Roarke was, from all accounts, a very unhappy woman."

I hadn't even known the lady, but I was forced to agree. Koestler had given me access to the file, which included photographs. Mrs. Roarke was a pale, thin, middle-aged woman with light eyes and a dispirited face that hinted at a brief and very transitory bloom.

"According to the family, she had left her home on two separate occasions previous to this." Koestler indicated Mrs. Roarke's photograph with a forefinger. "Not the sort of woman you'd expect to have problems sleeping, but she was quite the insomniac. Took drives at night to calm her nerves."

"Interesting pastime in the middle of a war. Gas rationing not apply to her?"

Koestler shifted uncomfortably. "The, uh, Roarkes are rather wealthy. If you take my meaning."

I did. "So what do you want me for?" I'll admit, I was having trouble following the logic of his argument. If the claim was payable, then the claim was payable, and that was that. Why bring in an investigator to prove what they already knew?

"Why, to investigate the claim, of course." Koestler's smile was very nearly roguish; it scared the hell out of me. "Thoroughly."

"You suspect something."

Koestler chuckled. "I'm in the insurance business, Frank. I suspect everything and everyone. If I didn't, Columbia would have long since gone bankrupt. No, it's my instinct that's giving me trouble on this one. It just seems too cut-and-dried for me, if you know what I mean."

"I do." His explanation made sense. "So we're disputing that she committed suicide? In favor of what? Murder?"

"I didn't say that." Koestler shot me a look. "Remember, the police found no body. Nor was a body found anywhere along the shore."

"Ever?"

He shrugged. "It's only been four days. It's not unusual for a body to be tugged under by the currents and not surface anywhere around here for months. When they do finally show up—"

"They're in Ireland?"

Koestler laughed. "Well, your geography is spot on."

"What about the dead woman's belongings—her purse, car keys, things like that."

"Nothing. Mrs. Roarke owned and drove her own car, a gift from her husband. She's had her driving license since she was sixteen. Never had an accident, never got so much as a parking ticket. Her husband claimed she'd driven up to the hill and jumped off, but according to the police, witnesses in the area would have remembered seeing a bright-red Chrysler Saratoga." He glanced at me. "There was no car, and certainly no tire marks, anywhere near where Mrs. Roarke supposedly jumped to her death."

"Huh. No car." The wheels in my head were clicking like lock tumblers. "Nobody found her purse... no car keys...." I was talking to myself.

"Nothing. She wore spectacles, but they weren't found at or near the scene."

"No glasses." This was key: suicide jumpers, for whatever reason, almost always took their glasses off—and although women were more likely to kill themselves with pills or in a self-inflicted vehicle accident, they seldom jumped to their deaths. "No glasses, no purse, no car, no Mrs. Roarke." I laughed. "You thinking what I'm thinking, Fred?"

"So it's fraud."

I shrugged. "Maybe."

We tipped down toward the city, the big car agreeably warm after the chilly blast on the outside. A destroyer was making its slow way into the harbor, aided by a tug on either side. The hills surrounding the city were still green and the water was a deep, almost navy blue. It wasn't New York, but maybe I could get used to it. Maybe, given enough time, I could even grow to like it. It didn't have the cachet of New York, didn't have New York's endless blocks of skyscrapers shutting out the sky, and perhaps most importantly of all, it didn't have Sam Lipinski, but maybe I could come to think of it as home.

I figured the place to start was with the family in question, so I got the address from Koestler and looked up the location on a city map. The Roarke family lived in what could only be termed a mansion, set back from the street in its own cozy little garden in the city's older and more prosperous section. The house was a huge, rambling wooden affair located on Kings Bridge Road. I presented myself at the door bright and early the next morning, fully expecting to be given the go-by.

"Are you the man from the gas company?" She was tall and slender, with a wealth of dark-auburn hair spilling down her back. I was pretty sure her dress was real silk, and her stockings too. The legs she came by honestly, courtesy of Mother Nature. She wore very little paint, merely a touch of lipstick, just enough to set off features that were the favorable side of stunning. "Dad, the man's here from the gas company!" Her accent was local, but not entirely; I imagined I could hear Fifth Avenue in it somewhere. She had the sort of low, husky voice you often associate with movie actresses and ladies of the evening, a sultry voice with thrilling things in it. "We had Reg last time. They usually send Reg. I'm not sure why they'd send you."

"I'm not either." I handed her one of my cards, waited while she'd read it.

Her expression went from merely surly to supercilious in the extreme. "Insurance investigator." Her eyes flicked over me, a dismissive glance. "Mr. Frank X. Boyle. I'm Vivian Roarke." She tucked the card into the pocket of her skirt. "So the X is for what? To mark the spot?"

"I represent Columbia All-Risk. Your mother had a policy with our company." I figured it was best to be blunt with this girl. She wasn't the type who'd appreciate even the most well-intentioned euphemism. "The death benefit, as you probably know, is payable to your father."

"I think you'd better come in." Her expression said I'd also better wipe my feet.

She showed me into a sitting room furnished with the best and brightest of what modern design had to offer: plump, representative lush sofas upholstered in velvet, matching footstools, and a variety of highly polished little tables set at appropriate intervals around the room. A grand piano commanded the space to one side of the fireplace, itself a massive marble affair big enough for a grown man to stand upright in. "Please, sit down." She selected a cigarette from the box on the coffee table and offered one to me. I declined. "You aren't a Newfoundlander, Mr. Boyle." Her eyes were green, tilted upward at the corners—cat's eyes. She reminded me of a cat, all sleek and predatory. I figured she probably had a nice set of claws to match. "What are you doing here? I'd have figured you for a G.I. type, Mom and apple pie." She drew on her smoke. "Didn't bother enlisting? Figured it had nothing to do with you? Or are you content to merely sit it out?"

My answer died quietly at the back of my throat as a second girl came into the room. She was a lot younger than Vivian, and where Vivian's hair was dark red, this girl had a head full of titian curls. Her eyes were blue, artfully and heavily painted, and there was a spray of freckles across her small, turned-up nose. Her mouth was colored a brilliant scarlet. She appeared to glide around the room as if mounted on casters; it was the sort of walk you see in dancers or actresses, but I had a strong feeling this girl was neither. "Vivian, Dad's coming down now." She caught sight of me and rolled over to where I now stood, having risen when she came into the room. "Oh my. Who's little who are you?" It was a line stolen from a movie, I was almost sure of it—*Footlight Serenade* or *The Philadelphia Story*—delivered in a low, throaty voice she probably practiced in front of her bedroom mirror. She couldn't have been more than sixteen.

"This is Mr. Boyle." Vivian crushed out her smoke and rose. "Mr. Boyle is from the insurance company. He wants to talk about Mamma."

"About…." The girl's lower lip quivered. "About *Mamma?*" She turned to Vivian, her eyes full of tears. "The brute! The absolute scoundrel!" And she flew at me, her small hands balled into hard little fists.

"Hey! Watch it!" I managed to hold her off, but not before she had landed half a dozen stinging blows. "I just got out of the hospital, if you don't mind." Vivian caught hold of the girl and pulled her away. "You ought to put a leash on her." My heart was hammering in my chest and I was sweating. This girl was nuts.

"Felice, that's enough." Vivian steered her to an overstuffed chair and dropped her onto it. The girl covered her face with her hands and commenced sobbing. "Mr. Boyle, I'm sorry. My sister has been inconsolable since Mamma… died." She crouched beside the chair and murmured something to the younger girl, who nodded and sniffled and finally accepted a handkerchief. I felt like I was watching a carefully scripted performance, one that was being enacted solely for my benefit. "She'd like you to forgive her."

"It's fine."

A side door opened and a man deep in the throes of late middle age stepped through. He had a thin, hawklike face, a rather beaky nose, and a chin that disappeared into the deep wattles and folds of skin at either side of his neck. He was wearing a cardigan sweater buttoned in the front and a silk cravat at his throat, dark trousers, and bedroom slippers. "I told them I was only going to deal with Reg from now on," he said. He held out his hand. "You had best just leave me the work order and I'll call round and have them send Reginald over instead."

"Dad, this is Mr. Frank Boyle. He's from the insurance company." Vivian handed him my card and waited while he read it.

"I just have a few questions for you, Mr. Roarke." I opened my briefcase and took out the sheaf of insurance papers Fred Koestler had given me. "Once we're satisfied that the conditions of the policy have been met, we'll release the check."

Roarke looked from Vivian to me and back again. His mouth trembled, and I wondered if he, like Felice, was about to burst into tears. He seated himself in a wingback chair and clasped his hands together in his lap. "It's a terrible going on, Mr. Boyd."

"Boyle," I corrected him.

He glanced up as if surprised to see that I was still there. "What? Oh yes, Boyle. It's a terrible thing. My wife wasn't in her right mind, you know." Vivian moved to stand behind her father's chair, one hand placed protectively on the back. Her manner intimated her intention to shield her father, but her eyes, I noticed, never left me. "That's why we preferred a private funeral. I'm sure you understand. A lot less interference from the press that way. *The Daily News* are absolutely ridiculous for butting in where they aren't wanted. Almost like an American paper, you could say." This last was a dig at me.

"Mr. Roarke, I apologize in advance if some of these questions seem inappropriate or too personal. Please understand I don't seek to offend you in any way. This is merely company policy." I laid the papers I'd brought out on the coffee table. "You're probably familiar with most of these forms. The first three outline the details of your wife's policy, which, as you know, names you as beneficiary. The other two are release forms that I'd need you to sign, accepting the terms of the payment and officially closing out your wife's policy. However, before we can do any of that, I need to be certain that Mrs. Roarke's death is…." This was the part I hated the most, and it was perhaps the most necessary. "Official."

Vivian Roarke's carefully tended reserve faltered, and her artfully painted lips thinned. "Official?" The husky voice seemed to drop an octave or two. "Are you saying you think my mother faked her own death in order to… what? Collect money from you?"

"Vivian!" Roarke snapped. "Mr. Boyle is only doing his job!" He rummaged in his cardigan pocket for a pipe and a pouch of tobacco. "I am sure Mr. Boyle understands how unpleasant this is for all of us and only wishes to expedite matters."

So, I thought, it's this old game. "That's correct." I took out my notebook and flipped to a clean page. "Mr. Roarke, had your wife been despondent in the days and hours leading up to her death? Had she, for instance, said that she planned to kill herself?"

Felice gave way to a fit of noisy sobbing and ran from the room. Vivian Roarke's hand tightened on the back of the chair.

"My wife was a very troubled woman, Mr. Boyle." Roarke filled his pipe and lit it. "She was often prey to fits of what you might call melancholy. We tried everything we could to help her: books, music, the theatre, trips to New York and abroad. Nothing helped."

"I see. I'm sorry to hear that." I drew a series of circles in my notepad. "Had your wife ever tried to commit suicide before?"

Roarke exchanged a look with Vivian. If my instincts were right, now they'd begin to fill in the blanks, giving me the background. This was usually when people let their imagination do the talking. Some of them enjoyed playing amateur psychologist.

Don't ever let 'em bullshit you, Charlie Blackwell had told me, way back in my early days, when I was still learning the business from him out in San Francisco. *Every goddamn thing comes outta their mouths is crap. Most people will lie to you for the hell of it.*

"My mother was very ill, Mr. Boyle." Vivian moved to the sofa and sat down, hands folded demurely in her lap. "She'd been to many doctors. Nothing helped." She glanced out the window, her expression appropriately bleak. "Dad did his best to protect her from herself, but in the end…." She shrugged. "I hope this satisfies you."

It didn't even come close to satisfying me, but I remembered the conversation I'd had with Fred Koestler on Signal Hill and rose to go. "Thank you for your time, both of you." I stuffed the papers back into my briefcase. "I hope I haven't upset you unduly."

Felice was waiting for me in the foyer. She'd dried her hysterical tears and repaired her makeup. She offered me a trembling smile. "He's done very well for himself this war, Dad has."

I wondered what she was driving at. "I suppose. That's good, isn't it?"

She slipped an arm through mine. "I didn't mean it when I hit you. I hope I didn't hurt you."

I disengaged her arm and stepped away. "I'm a big boy. I think you'll find I can take care of myself."

"He's not what everybody thinks he is, my father." Her voice was a loud hiss that must have carried for miles. "You'll find out. Everybody thinks he's such a patriot, a philanthropist—"

The girl was suddenly and decisively yanked away from me. Vivian had come to protect her family's honor yet again. "You'll have to forgive my sister." Her green eyes were like pieces of sea glass: depthless, hard, and brittle. "She doesn't know what she's saying."

The last glimpse I had of the Roarke house was much the same as the first, only this time Felice Roarke was seated in an upstairs window, her hand pressed hard against the glass. I wondered what she was trying to tell me.

Chapter Three

SERGEANT ALPHONSUS PICCO wasn't the sort of cop whose time you feel comfortable wasting. I was pretty sure nobody in his right mind would ever waste anything of Sergeant Picco's, if he valued his life. The headquarters of the Royal Newfoundland Constabulary were located in Fort Townsend, at the top of a steep and treacherous hill that immediately called to mind my days in San Francisco. Figuring I could use the fresh air and exercise, I decided late one afternoon to walk up from my Water Street office, and by the time I got there, I was winded but good. My inquiries at the front desk resulted in my being shown down a narrow, poorly lit hallway to Sergeant Picco's office, where I waited for close to half an hour before the sergeant appeared. He was young—a lot younger than I'd been led to expect—and he had the kind of wan beauty I'd often seen in the men around here. His eyes were pale, and his light-brown hair was carefully cut and combed to one side. He couldn't have been more than thirty.

I introduced myself and offered my hand. "Frank Boyle. I'm with Columbia All-Risk. I understand you're the officer assigned to the Roarke case?"

He straightened his uniform tunic before he sat down. "I'm Sergeant Picco."

"Oh." I couldn't resist. "Maybe you won't mind if I... picco your brain?"

"How funny," he said flatly. "I've never heard that one before." He flipped open a file folder that was sitting on his desk and began leafing through it. "I'll have a copy of my report messengered to your office. Good-bye."

"Now wait just a minute—"

"Mr. Doyle—"

"Boyle."

"Mr. Boyle, I have a lot of work to do. As far as I'm concerned, the Roarke case is open-and-shut. Mrs. Roarke jumped off Signal Hill. The body was never found. Good-bye." He bent to his reading again.

"You know, it's a wonder you guys get anything done around here." I stood up, the blood pulsing in my temples. "I figured we could work together, maybe pool our resources, but you're more interested in that stupid file folder there in front of you! What's so important, anyway? You reading the funny papers? Or maybe it's a girlie magazine."

Picco stood up. All the blood seemed to have drained from his face except for two bright-red spots burning high up on his cheekbones. His pupils were huge, and his lips pressed tight against his teeth. When he spoke, his Irish accent was pronounced and he enunciated each word carefully. "Last night the body of Augustus Quigley, who had been missing from his home for three months, was found floating in the water adjacent to the American dock." He drew a shuddering breath. "You'll forgive me if all my… faculties aren't readily at your disposal." He sat down heavily. There was a long, quivering silence in the room, a silence that seemed to stretch and bend, a silence like a living thing.

"I'm sorry."

His pale eyes came up to meet mine.

"No, really, I am. I apologize."

He gazed at me, trying to decide whether I meant it. "I'm busy. Get out."

"Sergeant, I could really use your help on this. I don't like this any better than you, but I have a job to do. It's not a job I asked for, but it is mine and I've got to see it through to the end." I sighed. "Please." I wondered why in God's name I'd bothered coming up here. Clearly he wasn't interested in helping me, only in getting me out of his office as quickly as possible. "I'm new around here... I just moved here from New York, and I don't know anybody. I don't believe Mrs. Roarke committed suicide. Every instinct tells me otherwise."

Picco's pale eyes shifted away from mine, and I knew there was more going on than he was telling. "Yes, the Roarkes." He shifted the file folder back and forth, smoothing his palm over the cover. "You're investigating the Roarkes." He wasn't quite distracted; this was something else.

"I am."

He reached behind him and opened the middle drawer of his filing cabinet, then handed me the folder he pulled out. "Some background information on the Roarke family, but I'm afraid there's not much there that'll be helpful to you." He shrugged. "They're a closemouthed bunch. They don't mix with nobody, and they don't talk to nobody. It's them to themselves."

I paged through it. He was right. The folder contained just a handful of typed pages and maybe half a dozen short features clipped from the local newspapers. "This is all you got?"

"That's all I got."

I thanked him and moved to go. At the door I stopped and turned back momentarily. "Do you think Mrs. Roarke killed herself, Sergeant?"

"What I think is none of your business."

"Like that, huh?" Something else occurred to me. "Sergeant, the place where Mrs. Roarke supposedly jumped over the cliff... have you or your men examined the site thoroughly?"

"Yes, we have examined it thoroughly." His tone said I was little better than an idiot for even asking such a question.

"It's just that…. I used to be a private detective before I got into the insurance racket. I dunno, you get a feeling for this sort of thing. I notice stuff." *You keep your goddamn nose to that grindstone and don't you dare bring it up 'til you have an epiphany.* Charlie had drilled it into me: *notice what nobody else does.* "There's only one set of perfect footprints—too perfect, if you ask me."

Picco's brows arched. "What do you mean?"

I frowned. "Just what I said. Anyway, I'm sure your men have been over the area." If there had been any footprints, they would be hopelessly obliterated by now, thanks to the trampling feet of the local constabulary.

He laughed nastily. "And you got the face to call yourself a detective." He took a cigarette out of a pack lying on the desk and lit it. I half expected him to blow the smoke in my face, the way people did in the movies.

"Insurance investigator." I was beginning to hate Sergeant Picco. "Would it be all right if I revisited the scene? I noticed it's been cordoned off."

"Sure, what do I care? Fill your boots, boy." He waved at the door, effectively dismissing me. Yes, I was pretty sure I hated Sergeant Picco, and by now, it was becoming clear that I'd get little or no help from the Royal Newfoundland Constabulary. That left me and the Roarke family, and I was pretty sure I was beginning to hate them too. They weren't in the mood to do me any favors, and by the time I'd finished my investigation—

"Whoa there! Mind how you go."

The voice was deep, mellifluous, more Irish than Picco's, and very masculine. I looked up into cornflower-blue eyes and a face that—to borrow a particle of Irish parlance—would make the angels weep. He was wearing a constabulary uniform, but where Picco's looked like his had come from Stores, this one had been professionally tailored and it hung on him like a dream. He was tall, maybe six feet, broad shouldered, and blond, and looking at him made a funny little flare of lust ignite inside my gut. I'd been so sunk in my own musings I'd nearly walked into him.

"Sorry," I said. "I ought to look where I'm going."

"New York, aren't you?" He held out his hand. "Eamonn Molloy."

I shook it. "Frank Boyle." His grip was strong, and his hand warm. He was just too beautiful to be real. "I guess the Newfies are recruiting outside the country these days—or maybe you're from another part of the island?"

He grinned. "You've got a great ear for accents and dialects, so you do. No, I'm from Kilgarvan, County Kerry. The constabulary recruited me from the Garda. They lost their old chief to the army."

"You're the Chief of Police." It was like a window opening to a warm spring day. "I'm so glad to meet you... you can't imagine."

"And I'm glad to meet you, Francis Xavier Boyle."

"You've been checking up on me."

"Not just you, but everybody who comes to town these days. I like to keep a hand in." His gaze swept over me, and something flickered in his face, something hot and elastic, something secret. He leaned close to me, gently gripping my elbow. "I wouldn't mind continuing this little chat of ours. I know a place that serves a decent whiskey. Are you game?"

THE Duke of Duckworth was one of those pubs that look almost indecently enchanting in the dark. Located down one of the sloping city laneways, it was the perfect place for a quiet drink or two. Besides the bar staff, there were only two other patrons, a couple of old men in tweed caps sitting in the corner and discoursing in their impenetrable Newfoundland brogue over a game of dominoes.

Eamonn Molloy signaled the barman. "Give us a wee dram of the Macallan, Brian." He had changed out of his constabulary uniform into a dark-blue suit with a warm gray topcoat and a navy snap-brim fedora. When he reached to add a little water to his whiskey, I saw the gleam of gold cufflinks and suddenly my gray workaday suit seemed rather shabby.

"Macallan?" If he meant to impress me, he'd succeeded. "Not to be indelicate, but how much are they paying cops these days?"

He grinned. "No trouble to tell you're an American, Frank. Everything's to have a dollar value."

"All right, so tell me about Kilgarvan." We were sitting at a booth in the back of the pub, listening to the faint strains of the bartender's radio and sipping a whiskey that, for all I knew, might as well have been distilled gold. I couldn't take my eyes off him; I realize that's a cliché, but it was the truth. He was one of the most striking men I'd ever seen, with that masculine beauty that is all strength and fire, muscle and steel.

"Tell me about New York," he countered, and we both laughed.

"I grew up in the Bronx," I said. "Hardly glamorous."

"What are you doing here in St. John's, then? Is there not enough detecting to be doing in New York?" He leaned over the little table, so small our knees were touching underneath it. I could feel the heat of him and smell the subtle scent of his aftershave lotion.

"I had to leave New York." I didn't feel like elaborating. "In a hurry, as it turns out."

"Did you?" He drained his whiskey and signaled the barman for another. "Why? Did you do something bad?" His grin was infectious. "Did you get some girl pregnant? Did her da come after you with the gun, now?"

"Nothing like that."

"The Mafia?" The barmaid laid two glasses down on our table, and Eamonn gave her a silver dollar—a sizeable tip, even if this wasn't wartime. "Isn't that what you fellows from the Bronx do? Get into trouble with the mob?"

He was teasing and I didn't mind. In fact I was enjoying myself. It had been a long time since I'd had someone to laugh with. "Would you believe me if I told you I'm hiding from the Camorra?"

He roared with laughter. "Ah, Frank, for the love of God, you're the worst liar I've ever met." He tasted his whiskey and added a little water. "But honestly now, why were you pestering poor Sergeant Picco?"

I explained the situation with the Roarkes, including my role in the investigation. "There's something about the whole thing that doesn't ring true," I said. "It's too tidy for a suicide. In my experience death is a messy affair."

He gazed at me, not without compassion. "Know something about that, do you?"

"Yeah." I wasn't ready to give him my whole history, not yet. "So what's your opinion? Did she do it herself, or did she have help? I notice no body's been found."

Eamonn thought for a moment while the two old men murmured over their dominoes. Somebody had dropped some money in the jukebox, and Bunny Berigan's big band was making short work of "I Can't Get Started." "Well, the currents and tides around these parts will often take a body out to sea. Picco said the same thing as you, though: it looks too much like a setup."

"Picco?" My ears felt like they were standing out on stalks.

"Oh, he's as sharp as a tack, that one."

"Are we talking about the same man?"

Eamonn leaned in close to me. "Let's not talk about him at all. He's not nearly as interesting as you are." His gaze was focused, intense. "Tell me about yourself, Francis Xavier Boyle. Tell me about New York, about the streets where you played as a wee boy. Tell me everything."

We stayed in the Duke until last call, and then Eamonn walked me back to Water Street. The city was silent and unaccountably dark because of the blackout, and it felt as if we were two intrepid explorers braving some unknown land. We consciously kept a slow pace, our arms linked, and now and then Eamonn would squeeze my arm with his.

"Would you look at that?" He nodded toward the full moon. "That's bloody gorgeous, that is." We took the long flight of stairs down by the courthouse, singing a filthy counting song Eamonn said he'd learned at school and laughing when we got it wrong. The good whiskey was singing in my veins, and I wasn't lonely anymore; I had a friend. "They'll think us a couple of drunk soldiers if we don't shut up," Eamonn said. We turned right and continued up Water Street, taking our time on the empty sidewalks. The moon provided enough illumination for me to see his face but no more. He might have been a genial ghost or some other creature of legend who'd agreed to be my escort for this night only.

"Thanks for walking with me," I said. We were at my door now, and my keys were in my hand, and it seemed boorish not to invite him up, so I did. I spooned a little of my preciously rationed coffee into the pot and set it on the stove, then put out cups and saucers. It reminded me of being in New York with Sam, sitting at his kitchen table in the companionable warmth of his apartment, the windows obscured by cooking steam, the radio playing "Fools Rush In." "I don't really know anybody here—it gets a bit lonely. I expect you know what I mean."

"That I do." Eamonn sipped his coffee and made a face, then tried to cover it.

"Too strong?"

"Oh no, it's perfect. It's lovely. See?" He reached for the sugar tongs and added three more lumps. "You Americans make it quite strong. I'm not used to anything being as strong, not even my whiskey."

I opened my mouth to say something when there was a sudden loud buzzing noise and every light in the place went out. "Oh for crying out loud!" I felt my way to the kitchen cupboards and fumbled for the matches. "The electricity's gone."

"Leave it." He was behind me, his body so close I could feel the heat of him burning through my clothes. "Jesus God, Frankie, do you know what sort of a place this is?" He spoke urgently, as though running out of time, and I wondered what made him feel this way. "A man like myself has to be careful…. He has to be so very, very careful." Still standing behind me, he eased my shirt free of my trousers and laid his warm hands on my naked skin. "Beautiful, you are."

My whole body was suddenly suffused with blood. "Eamonn, what—"

"Sh. Never you mind." His questing fingers slid into the front of my trousers, unerringly finding my cock, and I moaned aloud, my head falling back onto his shoulder. He worked me like an expert, sliding the elastic skin of my erection slowly over my swollen length while his strong arm held me against him.

"Gonna come." I had barely time to say anything at all: my completion roared through me like a tidal wave, hollowing me out inside. I turned in his arms and our open mouths met in a searing kiss, and then I was on my knees in front of him, hauling his cock out. He grunted when I sucked him into my mouth, and he muttered something incoherent as his fingers found their way into my hair. I gave him every trick Nicky Brooks had ever taught me, and by the time I finally let him come, he was trembling. I took my mouth away, and with one final tug, I pulled him over the edge, his big chest rising and falling in a hectic rhythm. The lights came on with a click and a sudden flare, illuminating us, the room, and everything.

"Ah, Jesus… ah Jesus, fuck—" He panted hard, his body shuddering down to sanity, and by the time he'd regained himself, we were both sitting on the kitchen floor, our backs pressed against the wall by my front door. "You give a good suck, Frankie." He caught the point of my chin in his hand and kissed me, then slowly rose to his feet. "I guess you got something on me, now, haven't you?" His tone was jovial, but I suspected he wasn't really kidding.

"Eamonn, I—"

"Sure, I'd better be going." He tucked himself away, straightened his clothes, and tidied his hair, all without meeting my eyes. "Getting later than I thought." He reached out and stroked my cheek. "Let's keep this between our two selves, okay?"

"Sure."

His expression was taut, strain showing in his eyes. I had the strangest sense he regretted what we'd just done. "I'll be talking to you, Frankie. Later on, huh?"

And just like that, he was gone.

I'D BEEN taking my meals at a local restaurant called the Heartache Café, and what Jack Stoyles, the owner, didn't know about the locals wasn't worth finding out. Over the course of a week's worth of lunches and suppers, he told me a lot about the Roarkes: how they were an old, established Newfoundland family with ties to England and Ireland and more than one stain on the old escutcheon. The oldest daughter aspired to carry on in the grand tradition, but there wasn't any money, and the youngest daughter was a flighty, addlepated little nymphomaniac who'd been twice arrested for peddling contraband chocolate and stockings; in the second instance Picco had been the arresting officer and Felice had seen fit to shove her lily-white hand down his pants in the squad car. As far as anyone could tell, the whole family was nuts.

"Vivian has been pulled over more times than you could count, mostly for speeding. She borrows her old man's clothes to go driving. She thinks it makes her less likely to get noticed by the cops." Jack told me this one Wednesday afternoon, when I sat in his café reading the paper. "She's got some kind of fancy sports car that the old man bought her—had it shipped in from England for her birthday—and she's fond of taking it up Mount Scio Road with the throttle all the way open." He offered me the dessert menu, but I declined. "Bad idea around these parts. There are moose in the woods and they've got no compunction about jumping in front of a speeding car."

"Bad for the moose?" I sipped Jack's excellent coffee and allowed myself a grunt of satisfaction.

"Oh no—bad for the driver. A full-grown moose can weigh fifteen hundred pounds."

I tried to imagine it and couldn't. "But I thought Vivian was married and settled down. What's she doing still living at home with her parents? She's got to be at least thirty years old."

"She's given marriage the old college try, I can say that for her." Jack rested the coffeepot on the back of an adjacent chair. "Three... no, I lie. She's been married four times at last count. Without exception she's divorced every single one of them. This last poor schmuck was off one of the merchant marine vessels, but there was one guy—an American—who was some kind of small-time crook."

An image of Nicky Brooks flashed into my mind. "He wouldn't have been from the Bronx, would he?"

Jack thought for a moment. "You know, I kind of think he was." He changed the subject. "Old Mr. Roarke, now there's a slippery character. Word on the street is that he's some kind of black market bigwig, except nobody's been able to prove it. They seem to be doing a bit too okay, if you ask me. You'd never know there was a war going on, to look at them."

"Do you think Mrs. Roarke killed herself, Jack?" I've never gotten anywhere by being coy, and in my business, the questions you probably shouldn't ask are usually the ones that get the answers.

"I dunno." He smiled thinly. "Did she?"

"Oh, you're piles of help."

Jack winked at me. "Thought you only came here for my coffee?"

"You're right." I grinned at him and tossed some money on the counter.

As soon as I stepped outside, a longshoreman the approximate size and thickness of a brick wall barred my path to the street. He was joined by a second man, so like the first in manner and appearance they could have been twins. The first one—a hulking behemoth with shoulders like barn doors—gave me a friendly toss into the side of an adjoining building. I hit the wall so hard I saw stars. "Where is she?" His rancid breath wafted across my nostrils like a foul wind.

"You have onions for breakfast?" I tasted blood and the recoil nearly snapped my neck.

"Don't play smart. Where's Velma?"

I struggled, but he was freakishly strong, and he had me good. "I don't know any Velma."

"Oh, you're going to be the laughing boy, are you?" His teeth resembled a row of rusty nails, and that grin was going to give me nightmares for months. "I saw you talking to the old man. He took her away somewhere, didn't he?"

"Look, buddy—I don't know anybody called Velma."

When he plunged his fist into my gut, all the air went out of my lungs. My vision started to get dark around the edges. I tried to speak but couldn't, and I figured this was it: my opportunity to die a stupid death. The sidewalk came up to meet me, about as friendly as it always is.

"Hey!" The voice was familiar. A pair of shiny black boots interrupted my view of the grimy sidewalk. "What's going on here? Don't you men have work?"

Sergeant Picco. I would have thanked him on my knees, if I could have gotten to my knees.

"We're not bothering you," the first one said.

Picco reached for the cuffs on his belt. "Do you want me to arrest you? Move along." He jerked his head at the HEARTACHE CAFÉ sign. "This is a place of business." He watched them go, then bent to address me. "Are you hurt?"

I accepted a hand up and painfully brushed myself off. "Thanks. Lucky you came along when you did. Those two were going to give me the full Broderick, there."

"I have no idea what you're talking about." He cast a disparaging glance over my appearance. "Move along, Mr. Boyle. You're cluttering up the sidewalk."

The café door swung open, and I heard Jack call, "*Chris, your boyfriend's here.*" Then the door swung shut and I was on the outside.

WHAT Jack had told me was swirling around in my mind the next morning when I went to see the Roarkes, and I wondered what other dirty laundry was hidden in their Kings Bridge Road mansion.

Mr. Roarke himself answered my knock. He assessed me warily, finally consenting to let me in when I flashed my credentials in his face. "I don't see how this is necessary, Mr. Boyle, any of it. Why you persist in forcing yourself on us—"

"Mr. Roarke, I'm here in my official capacity as the investigator assigned to your claim. Now, if there's anything about that you don't understand, I'd be happy to explain it to you." Some part of me wanted him to challenge me so I could try out my hypothesis of fraud. I wanted to see what would happen if I outright asked him whether or not his wife was actually dead and not just faking, as I suspected.

He sighed in an exaggerated manner, and I could see where the youngest daughter got it. "All right. What do you want?"

There was a flutter of movement just inside the door and Vivian appeared, still clad in her dressing gown and smoking a cigarette. Even at this early hour—just past nine—her hair was beautifully coiffed and her makeup was impeccable. "Back to torment us again, Mr. Boyle? Perhaps a call to your immediate superior might be in order."

"Good morning to you, too, Miss Roarke. Are you content that I have a reason to be here, or shall I wave my license under your nose as well?" I wasn't in any mood for it. I'd slept badly, tormented all night by dreams of Sam, New York, and Nicky Brooks—and other things, things I thought I'd forgotten. The cufflink I'd found on my pillow at the Newfoundland Hotel still gave me serious pause.

She scoffed. "What do you want?"

She wasn't going to like it, but I didn't care. "I'd like to see your mother's room, if you don't mind. Columbia has authorized me to take a thorough inventory of its contents if I deem it necessary."

"I do mind. In fact, I mind very much." She drew hard on the cigarette and blew smoke through her nostrils. It wasn't an attractive thing to do.

"That's unfortunate, but I'm afraid I can't direct the company to release the check to the beneficiary until my investigation is complete." I smiled. "Of course, it's entirely up to you. I'm still getting paid. In fact, I'm on the clock right now." I made a show of checking my watch.

"I don't know why you couldn't have done this on your previous visit," Vivian said. She jerked her head in the direction of the stairs. "I'll show you." She laid a hand on her father's shoulder. "Dad, you go on and finish your breakfast. I'll take care of Mr. Boyle."

I followed her dressing gown up a curving set of sumptuously carpeted stairs and down a hallway whose rugs dragged on me like a Florida swamp. "My father suffers from migraine headaches," Vivian said. "He and Mother have slept apart for years."

"I think I got it," I replied. "'Not tonight, honey, I've got a headache'?"

She threw me a look over her shoulder. "You really are a disgusting man."

The mother's room was located at the end of the hall, in a part of the house that faced away from the street. There was a pervasive smell of mothballs but hardly any dust, which didn't necessarily mean anything. The bed had been made, the covers stretched taut over a high mattress, and the drapes were closed, shutting out the daylight. A pair of women's pink bedroom slippers had been placed side by side next to the night table, and a dressing gown, also pink, hung on the wardrobe's open door. I checked the wardrobe, feeling for a false back or a hidden compartment, but it contained only the sort of clothes you'd expect a middle-aged woman to own. I got down on my hands and knees and looked under the bed, but the dust was undisturbed. The dresser boasted a silver brush and comb set with a matching hand mirror and powder box, all in the same pattern, and a vase of red roses, their blossoms dry and long since dead, dropped small green leaves onto the white bureau scarf. Just for the hell of it, I lifted the vase and felt the bottom of it: bone dry. The water inside was brackish and full of green scum. The flowers had been there for some weeks. Nobody had used this room for quite a while. "When did you last see your mother, Miss Roarke?"

"Oh, for God's sake!" She clenched her fists. "The day before she died, Mr. Boyle. The day before my mother died." She stubbed out her cigarette in a convenient ashtray and came to where I was. "Clearly you've concocted some notion, but why, I have no idea."

"There is just one set of footprints on the hill—no hesitation marks, nothing. Do you know how unusual that is? Most suicides rehearse it a couple of times before they actually go over the edge. She might have walked back and forth. People usually do. She would have taken off her glasses, her shoes, maybe her gloves, and left them at the scene."

"Her gloves?" At this proximity, her face revealed her true age. There were tiny lines running from the corners of her eyes, lines bracketing her mouth. She could have been something approaching pretty if she relaxed a little and stopped trying so hard to be competent and tough. "Her shoes?"

"When... forgive me... when a person commits suicide by jumping, they rehearse it for a while. But once they've decided, people at that stage don't change their minds. They take that last leap, and believe me, Miss Roarke, some of them take it running." I watched her face carefully, but there was no change in her expression. I might as well have been talking about the weather. "It's just a theory." I shrugged. "Skip it."

"So you do think she killed herself. Is that what you're saying?" She fastened onto this idea eagerly—a little too eagerly.

"I'm not saying anything. It was just a theory." I glanced at my watch. "Thank you for this. I'm afraid I'll have to be going now." And I started down the stairs. In the living room, I stopped and took a good, long look at the ceiling. Was Mrs. Roarke hiding in some attic room, like the mad wife in a Gothic novel? And if she was, what then?

THE Roarkes' next-door neighbors lived in a large yellow house whose grounds encompassed at least half an acre. The house itself boasted medieval-style turrets, each surmounted with its own weathervane, and I counted no less than six chimneys rising out of the roof. A huge beech tree grew next to the front door, which was inset with cut glass that gave back the morning sunlight in a dazzling display. The lawn and the remnants of a small rock garden sparkled under a thin coat of hoarfrost, and the air smelled fresh and cold. An elderly man in corduroys and a cardigan answered my knock; he held a teacup in one hand and a piece of toast in the other. "Come in, young man, come in." He waved me into a dark-paneled foyer smelling pleasantly of lemon oil. "Now, which one are you? The gasman or the electric? I can never remember."

I handed him my credentials. "I'm with Columbia All-Risk. I'm investigating the death of Mrs. Roarke, your neighbor. Would you mind if I asked you a few questions?"

"Frank Boyle." He handed my wallet back to me. "What does the X stand for?"

I couldn't help but laugh. "It's Xavier," I said. "Francis Xavier Boyle, but most people call me Frank."

"I am Elijah Temple." He took my arm companionably and drew me into the front room. "Most people call me Lije. Do you know, Mr. Boyle, I am ninety-two years of age? Oh, yes. I should be dead, but I'm not, and every day I'm thankful for that." He showed me to the couch and sat down himself in a leather wingback chair. "I spend my days in the company of my granddaughter, Lois, and mostly I read or do a little gardening. You ought to come back in the summer, Mr. Boyle—the Cabot roses are simply spectacular."

"I'd like that."

"An American, aren't you?" He scrutinized me keenly, and I decided anybody who underestimated Mr. Lije Temple would be the worst kind of an idiot. "From New York, if I'm not mistaken."

"You got me, Mr. Temple." I grinned. "I grew up in the Bronx."

"Mr. Boyle, I am in the middle of my breakfast. I wonder if you would join me. Lois would be only too happy to prepare something."

It had been hours since I'd eaten a piece of toast and drunk a cup of coffee, and investigation work always made me hungry, but I didn't think it would be good manners to accept. "I appreciate it, Mr. Temple, but—"

"Young man, I shall be very put out if you don't join me." His pale-blue eyes said he would brook no argument. I had no other choice but to give in, and within moments, a young woman—pretty, in a pale sort of way—appeared from the kitchen bearing a silver tray laden with a coffeepot and all sorts of dainties. She laid the tray carefully down on the coffee table. "You must try the cake. Lois will be crushed if you don't. After all, it was this cake that compelled Danny Roarke to ask Lois for her hand."

The girl was clearly embarrassed. "Poppy, that was a long time ago." She had the same kind of Irish accent as her grandfather and the Roarkes.

"Danny Roarke? He's related to the Roarkes next door?" I tried the cake. It was delicious. "And you were engaged to him."

"Yes, if you can call it that." Mr. Temple's face had hardened into set lines of old anger. "Danny is one of the Roarke cousins. That whole family is so tangled you can't tell one end from the other. There was another one of them, Jim Roarke, who spent most every summer up fishing on the Labrador, or so he said. Bloody scapegrace, that's what he was. Not fit to wipe your boots on."

"Poppy, don't—you know what the doctor said." Lois reached to pour coffee for both of us. "Don't be getting your blood up."

"That Roarke—that bloody—Lois, no decent woman should hear this sort of talk. Go on out into the kitchen." He waited 'til the girl had left the room. "Let me tell you something about the Roarkes, Mr. Boyle. They can smell a dollar for miles. Handy Roarke came over here in 1807, when this island was nothing more than a rag-taggle collection of fish merchants at each other's throats. He figured Newfoundland was a good place to make a killing, and he was right. It was only twenty years later when the Roarkes owned five schooners, and them going back and forth to the Labrador all summer long. That was back when cod was king, of course." The old man paused to take a sip of his coffee. "It was said—and I've no reason to disbelieve it—that Handy Roarke's crowd would rob the pennies off a dead man's eyes in full view of the mourners and not think anything of it. They were that brazen. Brazen as brass, the whole works of them. Anyway.

"My youngsters and the Roarke youngsters grew up together. Rodney and Vivian used to knock around with most of the Roarke cousins. My Rodney—that's him in the picture up there." He pointed to a photograph of a sober-faced young man in the uniform of the Royal Newfoundland Regiment. "He died at Beaumont-Hamel with the rest of them. You know about Beaumont-Hamel, the Battle of the Somme? Do they teach that in your history books, down in New York City?"

I suppressed a smile. "Yes, sir, they do."

"Well, my Rodney and Danny Roarke's father, Jim, were best buddies. When war broke out in 1914, they even joined up together." He paused to draw a long breath, and it seemed to me something went out of him, some fury or resolve. "Yes, well." He pushed away his plate, the rest of his food uneaten. "The way I heard it—and I don't know if it's right—is that Rodney and Jim were in the trenches with Harry Batten, another young fellow they were at school with. They all went to St. Bon's. Do you know St. Bon's?"

I recalled passing by the elegant building on Bonaventure Avenue, once a Franciscan seminary, shortly after I'd arrived. Fred Koestler had seen to it I'd had a thorough tour of the city. "Sure."

"Anyway, Rodney and Jim were having a smoke before they went over. Rodney only had the one match left, and he struck it to light for the three of them. He lit his cigarette and then Harry's, and of course, Jim was left for last."

"Three on a match." I was familiar with the superstition. "That's bad luck."

"Right you are, sir. Three on a match."

"That was it for him. He was done. The order was given, and they were just hoisting themselves over the lip of the trench when a stray bullet came out of nowhere. Jim was hit in the face. The bullet took out his right eye, his ear on that side, and most of his cheekbone. Oh no, he wasn't dead. Not by a long chalk." The old man shook his head. "But he'd never be the same again."

He didn't have to tell me. I'd seen photographs of men who'd had their faces and their lives torn apart in the Great War. I could just imagine the sort of reception young Roarke encountered on his return home.

"My Rodney died during the battle. A mine landed near where he was standing, and he was blown up." He turned to his coffee cup, then refilled it from the pot at his elbow. I sensed there was a lot of emotion roiling under the surface. "Jim Roarke shut himself up in the house when he came back, and he never went out again in the light of day. His young wife, a Shearstown girl he'd married before the war, lived there for a while, but she couldn't stand the seclusion, shut up in there all the time. She left young Danny with his grandparents and went home to her own people. I don't know if they ever got divorced or what. She never came back. As time went on, Jim Roarke got strange in the head. He figured people could see him even when he was inside the house, so he hired Bob Buffett over in Rabbittown to build him a secret room somewhere in the house, nobody knows where it is. They found him in there a few years ago. The doctor figured he'd done away with himself."

"Was this the family doctor?"

Old Mr. Temple nodded slowly. "Yes. Yes, I believe it would be. That was Doctor Nichol—old Doctor Nichol, mind you. He died not too long ago, but his son took up the practice after his father passed on."

I jotted this down in my notebook. "And this young Doctor Nichol, does he maintain a practice here in town?"

He thought for a moment. "I believe he do," he said slowly. "Yes, I believe he do, but you'd better ask Lois. My memory isn't what it once was."

That made me smile. "Mr. Temple, you have a better memory than most men a third your age."

He waved it away. "The Roarkes blamed my Rodney—because of the three on a match, you see. It was his match. When they heard that Danny had asked Lois for her hand, they accused me of bringing pressure to bear. Called Lois all sorts of names, said they would have us in a lawsuit—you know, the usual thing."

"That's monstrous." But entirely typical. People always look around for somewhere to lay the blame. "So how did it all work out? The lawsuit, I mean."

"Oh, that." He smiled. "That's a story for another time."

I stood up and located my hat. "Mr. Temple, you've been of immeasurable help to me." I gave him my card. "If you ever need anything—anything at all—please get in touch with me."

"Well, that's right kind of you." He scrutinized the card with eyesight probably every bit as keen as his memory. "I got lots of insurance, but you never know. If I needs more, I'll give you a ring."

I went out into the kitchen and found Lois standing over a sink full of dishes. When she saw me, she turned off the taps and dried her hands on her apron. "Mr. Boyle. Are you taking your leave of us?"

She really was, I thought, a lovely girl, and what a shame she was left to languish here in what amounted to a luxurious cloister. Her grandfather was no doubt good to her, but I wondered what sort of life a girl her age could have, living here in relative seclusion. "I'm afraid so. Lois, I wanted to thank you for the coffee, and for your hospitality."

She blushed, a delicate diffusion of blood beneath pale skin. "Oh, Mr. Boyle. You're more than welcome."

"I wondered, too, if you could answer me a question."

"Of course. Anything at all, you've only to ask."

"Your grandfather mentioned that a young Doctor Nichol keeps a medical practice here in the city. I need to speak with him, in the interests of my investigation, you understand. Would you happen to know where his office is located?"

It was as if I had slapped her in the face. "You've got your nerve." Her hands clenched the hem of her apron 'til her knuckles showed white beneath the skin. "Who put you up to asking that? Me grandar?" She advanced on me, her body set and angry. "You think you know what you're talking about, but you don't know anything. You, coming up here from New York City, with your fancy suit and your polished shoes, asking questions about things that are none of your goddamned business." She reached behind her, into the dish drain, and picked up a heavy skillet, the likes of which I'd seen before. My mother had owned one, and I'd never forget the time she slammed it into my father's drunken face, nearly breaking his jaw. I didn't know why Lois was suddenly so angry, but I knew I didn't want to mess with her.

"I'm sorry. I didn't mean to offend you." I backed toward the door.

"Get out!"

I ducked onto the porch just in time to hear the heavy skillet connect with the door. Mr. Temple shouted from somewhere inside the house, but I didn't stay to hear what he was saying. I took to my heels and shot across the street to where a huge blue Victorian with innumerable turrets and towers crouched malevolently.

My knock brought a painfully thin middle-aged woman with her hair in a bun and a pair of silver pince-nez perched on her skinny snout. She invited me into the foyer but no further. The entire house smelled of mold and boiled cabbage. I showed my credentials. "Do you mind if I ask you a few questions? I'm investigating Mrs. Roarke's death for Columbia All-Risk Insurance."

She consented with something less than ravishing eagerness. "I don't know why people can't leave that poor woman alone."

"Well, it's in her interest," I said. "How well do you know the Roarkes?" A tortoiseshell cat appeared from one of the inner rooms and began winding itself around my legs. I like cats—animals in general are some of my favorite people—but he was getting hair all over my pants.

"I've lived here all my life." She peered at me through her tiny glasses, her thin, bloodless mouth compressed into a hard white line. "I know them very well. Better, in fact, than a great many people who are nowhere near their equals."

"Uh-huh." I took out my notebook and made a pretense of jotting this down, but her information was useless. *There's one in every crowd,* Charlie had often said, *always ready to give out with misinformation. It's like a sacred duty with them.* "Thanks for your help." I stepped away, shutting the door carefully before the cat could escape.

It had started to rain again, and I had no umbrella. As I made it to the street, a bus went by, splashing me with cold, dirty water. So far, this investigation had all the earmarks of a real pain in the ass. On the one hand, I had genteel, generous Mr. Temple, whose information gave me the first real lead I'd had on this case—his crazy granddaughter notwithstanding—and on the other hand, I had people like Snooty Pince-Nez, whose reverence for the *droit du seigneur* overrode any instinct she might have had to do the right thing. I was beginning to think I was the unwitting target of an episode of *Candid Microphone,* and that was when I saw him: a slender man, about my height, wearing a tan trench coat and a fedora. He was standing on the corner in front of St. Thomas's Church, looking intently in my direction like he knew me.

"Hey!" I started toward him, but just then, a second bus rumbled past, inches from the curb, and by the time it had passed, the man was gone.

Chapter Four

DOCTOR ELMER NICHOL maintained a modest medical practice in an equally modest redbrick building on Duckworth Street in the city's downtown core. The waiting room smelled of carbolic acid and wet wool. At this hour—just after nine on a rainy Friday morning—only a handful of people were in attendance. I presented my card to the receptionist. "I have an appointment with Dr. Nichol."

"Mr. Boyle!" He must have been hovering in the background—"lurking" would have been a better word—because he suddenly unfolded himself into the room, all six feet eight or nine inches of him. He was young, maybe twenty-five years old, and an absolute colossus of a man. Outrageously tall and ridiculously fit, his body was an imposing rack of bone upon which solid muscle had been generously sculpted. He was blond and blue-eyed, and reminded me of nothing so much as some ancient Nordic god come to earth. When he shook my hand, he nearly broke my bones. "I've been expecting you. Come on through."

We passed through the reception area and into a maze of narrow corridors and tiny doors. I followed Nichol's broad back into a sumptuously decorated office dominated by a huge oak desk and a full-length painting of a young woman in some sort of Halloween costume. "She's ready for a party," I observed, nodding toward the picture. The girl seemed vaguely familiar, but her face was partly hidden by the folds of the costume, so I couldn't tell if I knew her or not.

"Isn't she gorgeous?" He reached out and caressed the frame with both hands, as if he were thinking of embracing the painting. "Lovely to look at, delicious to hold…." He sighed, obviously caught up in some private reverie. "Ah, Mr. Boyle, love can make us suffer the torments of the damned."

It was an odd way to open the conversation, but I went along for the ride. "Sure." The girl in the painting was wearing men's trousers over a pair of men's rubber boots, but her top half was decorated with a voluminous floral dress that, when viewed from a certain angle, appeared translucent—so translucent that the swell of her creamy breasts enticed the eyes. She wore something on her head that might have been—I wasn't sure—a pillowcase. It had been pulled up slightly to reveal a lovely face, young and winsome, with big soft eyes and a spray of freckles across the nose. Her mouth was full, her lips slightly parted, and a subtle sheen of moisture gleamed on her chin and on the strong planes of her cheeks. She looked—as my old boss Charlie Blackwell used to say—as if she'd been rode hard and put away wet. The expression on her face was one of satisfaction, or voluptuous luxury. Whoever had painted the picture had obviously meant to convey an impression of frank sexual hunger. "That's quite a costume she's wearing."

"Mummers," he said, stepping away from the picture. "Are you familiar with the term?"

I searched my memory and came up with some vague images revolving around my father—drunk, as usual—and several of his work buddies, dressed up in old clothes at Christmastime with sheets over their heads or something. *Pour the lad a snort or two. It'll put hair on his chest.* I remembered being woken up and taken out of my bed in the middle of the night and brought blinking into the harsh light of our kitchen, where my father and his friends sat at the table with a bottle of rye and the radio up on bust. "Uh, kind of." I nodded toward the painting. "Friend of yours?"

"Only the light of my life, Mr. Boyle." He sat down behind the massive desk. "Only the light of my life. Now then, what can I do for you?"

I explained why I was there and what Mr. Temple had told me, leaving out, of course, the bizarre altercation with Lois in the kitchen. "Mostly I'm looking for background information on the Roarke family. I understand your late father was the Roarke family physician."

"Well, now, you've been doing your homework," he said cheerily. He pulled open his desk drawer and rifled through some files until he found what he wanted. "Dad was their doctor, that's true. Not that they ever had anything wrong with them. I never saw a healthier bunch in my life."

"Oh, I see."

He winked at me. "That's a fine kettle of fish, I can tell you." He flipped through the contents of the folder. "I wish I could help you, but I couldn't possibly divulge confidential medical information, you understand."

"Yes, I know that, but I was hoping you could give me some insight into the family itself. You see, I'm trying to uncover the facts as they pertain to an insurance claim."

"Mmm...." His tone was noncommittal. "I'd have to be very careful, Mr. Boyle. You see, I have to live in this community. I can't simply take my hat in my hand and go along my merry way."

In spite of myself, I bristled. "Is that what you think I'm doing?"

"Of course not." The smile was thin as a dime and worth about as much. "The Roarkes are a very well-established family. One doesn't simply smear such a reputation."

"Oh, for God's sake!" I stood up. "I'm sick and tired of this 'to the manor born' garbage. So the Roarkes have money. Big deal." I jammed my hat onto my head. "If that's all you can offer me, Doctor, it's worthless. I'm afraid I'm just wasting your time." I felt like he was giving me the bum's rush. "Good day." I headed for the door.

"Wait!" He caught my arm; it was like being mauled by a polar bear. "Don't misunderstand me, Mr. Boyle." He took a breath. "I'd be lying if I pretended that my dealings with the Roarkes were entirely in the way of business, you understand."

Now we were getting somewhere. "Oh?"

"You remarked on my painting." He gestured at the girl in mummers' garb. "Do you recognize her?"

I took another look and it suddenly gelled for me. "Felice Roarke."

He moaned quietly and shook his head. "The torments of the damned, Mr. Boyle, as I said. To be given a glimpse of Heaven just once and to be turned back once you were within the very gates."

"So she let you inside her gates?" I asked. "Now that doesn't surprise me."

He flushed. "Don't be a pig."

"So you and Felice Roarke are… what, exactly? Friends? Lovers?"

"I asked for her hand, but she refused me."

"That's hard to believe," I said, "considering what she consented to." I gazed pointedly at the painting. "It's pretty modest as far as modern art goes, but something tells me you've got other images, pictures that are maybe not so modest." I waited, but he said nothing. "Am I right, Doctor?" He swung, but I nailed him in the shins with my heel until he was level with me, then caught his arm and twisted it behind his back. He didn't make a sound when I shoved him into the wall. "I wouldn't try that again if I were you."

He struggled to free himself, sweating and red-faced. "You can't come around here asking those sorts of questions."

"I don't know what you mean." I let go of him, and watched as he straightened his clothes and patted that impeccable blond hair back into place. "I'm only trying to settle an insurance claim, Doctor. You're the one with the dirty pictures."

Some sixth sense—the kind I usually rely on to save my ass—tingled a warning, but I ignored it. I charged through the waiting room and stepped out onto the sidewalk when something hard and heavy, moving like the Super Chief on a downgrade, slammed into the back of my head. I went down, the rough concrete of the sidewalk searing a trail of agony into the left side of my face. *Shake it off*, I kept telling myself, but it was no good. The last thing I remembered was a pair of very shiny shoes stepping past me, right before the blackness dove in and covered me in silence.

I WOKE up lying on the stairs outside a pub. Some wag had decided I'd look more interesting upside down, so for a long time, I didn't know where I was. A waft of cigarette smoke and stale beer gingerly tickled my nostrils, and it felt like my back was broken. My head pounded in time with the beat of my heart, and I hissed a few choice epithets as I struggled to my feet. This whole getting-beat-up thing was starting to become a bit tired; I needed a new party trick.

At Prescott Street I stopped, waiting for the traffic cop to wave me through, and there he was again, the same man I'd seen on Kings Bridge Road: about my height, slender build, tan raincoat, and wearing a fedora with the brim tilted to cover most of his face. As far as tails went, he was pretty easy to spot. "Hey! Hey, you!"

He turned and started up Prescott Street, and I didn't wait for the cop. I plunged into morning traffic and took off after him, but he gave me the slip. *Twice in one day, kid.* I could almost hear Charlie's voice in my head. *You're a bit off your game, aren't you?*

I walked back down to Duckworth and waited this time 'til the cop gave me the go-ahead. He deliberately kept me waiting, waving me back to the curb while he let a long line of cars go by—but then I saw the purple ribbons and the wreaths and realized it was a funeral procession. The traffic going in the opposite direction had all stopped, and in deference to the mourners, the cop had removed his hat. I did the same and stood with bowed head until the cortege had passed. It reminded me of things I'd tried my hardest to forget, like the way my mother had died at home of a heart attack one day while I was working as a bookie's runner. I was sixteen years old. I came home and called out to my mother, but there was no answer, and then I saw her. She was dead, sitting in her chair, a pile of mending in a basket at her feet. People say the dead look like they're simply asleep, but my mother didn't look like she was sleeping. She looked dead. Her face was gray and all the warm life that had lived in her smile and her eyes was gone. I went to her on my knees, caught hold of her cold hands, and cried.

We had no money for a funeral, so I went to the local parish priest at St. Angela's to ask for help. *When was your mother last at mass? Hasn't it been months since she's even made her confession?* I told him it had been a while, but Ma was awful tired come Sundays, especially with looking after us and working like she did. *She should have given more thought to her immortal soul,* was all he said and turned away. I never set foot inside a church again.

I appealed to the guys at work and finally my boss, who passed word down the line that Frankie B's mother needed a funeral. I didn't want charity, but if that was what I had to do in order to give Ma a proper send-off, so be it. The boss got back to me soon after, told me not to worry, everything would be taken care of, and sure enough, within half an hour, a hearse pulled up to our place and two somber young men in black took possession of my mother's body and carried her respectfully out of the only home she'd ever known. Later that night, me and my sister, Mercy, and my little brother, Leo, got a phone call telling us where and when the funeral would be held. We didn't have to do anything at all, just show up in our Sunday best.

On the morning of my mother's funeral, a long, black car pulled up to the Bronx tenement where we lived. A uniformed chauffeur informed us he was there to take us to the funeral. Everybody on the street, everybody who knew Ma when she was alive, had turned out to see us and to watch the hearse go by. It was the biggest thing in my neighborhood since Joey Truffalo had been scouted by the Yankees.

Mercy kept asking me, "Frankie, where'd you get the money for this?" And when I told her to never mind, she said. "It's that guy you work for, that Nicky Brooks. I know what he is. Ma knew what he was. You should be ashamed of yourself."

I asked her when was the last time she rode in a car, and that shut her up for a while, but when we got back home, my older brother, Robbie, took me into the kitchen and told me to "Get it out of your head, Frankie. You got no business being involved with them in the first place."

He was right. It was my fault—and Nicky Brooks's fault— what happened to my little brother, Leo. It would always be my fault and Nicky Brooks's fault, until the day I died. That was just the way it was.

THE first time I heard the name Nicky Brooks, I was sixteen years old, working as a messenger boy for a bookie in the Bronx. I hadn't done real good in school, just enough to graduate, and I didn't know nothing about nothing. I was grateful for the three bucks a week I earned running messages for Cal "The Hoot" Marquese and the occasional two bucks a luckier-than-usual bettor might flip my way.

I was hanging around the shop one afternoon, waiting like the rest of the guys, when a big, shiny Packard pulled up in front and a man got out. He was dressed real fancy, in the kind of clothes you almost never saw in my neighborhood, with his overcoat slung around his shoulders and a fedora tilted over his left eyebrow. He seemed to be listening to some kind of private music as he walked, and it informed his step so he glided along to the beat of this inner melody, a slight smile playing about his lips. He was one of the handsomest men I'd ever seen in my life: slender, dark, and sleek like a predatory animal, with a long, straight nose and a sculpted mouth and the eyelashes that belonged on a dame. He was dressed to the nines, and he looked like a Sunday picnic in the park, and when he stopped to speak to me, I was so nervous I nearly wet myself.

"Hey kid, how's tricks?" And, when I didn't speak, he asked, "Cat got your tongue, huh? That's too bad. Cal around?"

"He's in the back room, Nick." One of the other boys spoke before I got the chance. "Says you should go right on in."

"Who's that?" I asked, once he had passed behind the counter and into the office. "I ain't never seen him around here before."

"That's Nick Brooks, you dumbbell." Tony Spumonte cast me a derisive look, but then Tony was always putting on the dog. "He owns this joint—this one and a lot of others. Don't you know nothing?" He gestured with his chin at the door Nick had just gone through. "He owns most of the Bronx, and what he doesn't own, he controls. Ain't nobody gonna get in Nick's way if they can help it. He's a real wise guy, that Nick."

I'd never heard of Nick, but I knew lots of guys just like him, back in my old neighborhood. He was the sort of bird who claimed a section of the city for his own, who took over corner stores and family-owned laundries and automats, converting them into fronts for various operations like bookmaking, prostitution, and bootlegging. Now and again some bigger, stronger guy with greater firepower or a politician in his pocket would come along and, after a lengthy and often bloody battle, oust his predecessor, and the whole shenanigans would start all over again. Yeah, I'd seen that sort of thing before.

I was sitting in the front of Cal Marquese's shop a few weeks later when the same big Packard pulled up in front and Nicky Brooks got out and went inside. I'd been up most of the night before, running messages for Cal, and by the time I finally got home, there was my paper route to do, so I was pretty tired. I guess maybe I'd been drifting a bit because I didn't notice when Nick sat down beside me.

"You tired, kid?"

I jumped up and started apologizing. I didn't want him to think he'd caught me sleeping on the job. I knew Cal would have no problem replacing me with some other guy, and I couldn't afford for that to happen. See, my old man had died a few years back, and it was up to me and Robbie to help Ma with the household and the younger kids, to bring the money in so we didn't end up in an orphanage or worse. Ma tried as hard as she could to keep body and soul together, taking in laundry and babysitting the younger kids in the neighborhood, especially the ones whose mothers worked in the factories and such. I'd promised myself I'd never be a burden on her, and so far, I'd made good on that promise.

"No need to press the panic button." Nick's dark eyes were full of mirth. "I just asked a question."

"I'm sorry, Mr. Brooks. It won't happen again."

"Cal working you too hard?"

"No, Cal's a great boss. I really like the work, and I'm awful grateful for the money. It's not like that at all, Mr. Brooks, I swear—"

He cut in, laughing. "No need to gild the lily, kid. I believe you."

I liked the way he looked when he laughed, and I realized he wasn't too much older than me—maybe ten years. His fingernails were manicured, and on the pinky finger of his left hand, he wore a gold ring with a real diamond in it. It had to be a real diamond; from what I'd heard about the man, Nicky Brooks wouldn't lower himself to wear glass. The tiny rubies in his cufflinks were real, and the stickpin in his tie was probably a diamond too. Just then Cal came out and told me to get my ass over to Westchester Avenue to collect. "You're sending him over to Westchester?" Nick asked. "By himself?"

Cal eased the cigar out of his mouth. "Yessir, Mr. Brooks. He goes everywhere by himself. He's a big boy, ain't he?"

Nick looked at me then, really looked me over. "Yeah," he said slowly, "I guess he is." He reached out and clapped me on the shoulder. "I'll be seeing you, kid."

I didn't think much about it at the time, but a couple weeks later, I came into work and Tony told me Cal wanted to see me in his office right away. "*He's* in there." I knew who he meant, and it made me scared. I needed this job. I couldn't afford to lose it, but I went in anyway.

Cal was sitting behind the desk with his usual cigar growing out the center of his mouth, and Nicky Brooks was there, perched on the edge and wearing a dark-blue chesterfield with a thin white stripe, the French cuffs of his shirt showing, blinding white. Looking at him made my mouth water, but back then, I didn't know enough to figure out why. My older brother worked part-time as an automobile mechanic while he studied accounting at night; my sister, Mercy, was still in school but planned to enter the convent as soon as she was ready. Nobody in my family had ever told me what it meant to look at a guy like Nick and feel something down deep that gnawed at my insides like thirst or hunger.

Nick stood up when he saw me, reached out his hand, and shook mine. "Frank! Frankie Boyle! Good to see you again. How've you been? How's your work?"

"I guess I do okay."

Nick glanced over his shoulder. "Hey, Cal, I think you can leave us alone for a bit. Close the door behind you. I'll let you know when I'm through."

Cal blinked at him—deliberately, like an animal—and chewed on his cigar. "But Nicky, I'm right in the middle of—"

"I said get out." Nick dusted my lapel with the flat of his hand and grinned at me. "Don't make me ask again, Cal." His tone was absolutely pleasant, polite, and civil, but there was menace underneath it, and I sensed Nick was one of those guys who did exactly as he said he would, every time. He waited 'til Cal had gone, and then he stood in front of me, so close that I could feel the heat of his body and catch the subtle waft of his cologne. His presence made me shake. "How much you make a week, kid?"

"Three dollars." I had to swallow. "And tips. Sometimes. If a guy's lucky."

He laid his hands on my shoulders, their heat burning through my clothes. "How'd you like to make a lot more than that?"

"Sure." His eyes were a brown so dark they were almost black, and there was a tiny mole just to the side of his nose. His lower lip was full and beautifully shaped, and seeing it reminded me of the things I did in my bed alone at night—things that made a wet spot on my mattress and gave me strange and fractious dreams.

"Can you slip your jacket off for me?" He walked around me, sizing me up, muttering to himself. He stood in front of me and ran his hands down my arms and felt my muscles. "Do you keep fit, Frank?"

"Yes, sir. I box a bit at Harry Lennox's gym and lift weights and run a little."

He laid his hands on my waist and probed my belly with his thumbs, feeling for my ribs. "You do sit-ups, stuff like that?"

"Some."

He laughed at this. "You're honest. I like that." He held out his hands. "Squeeze my hands, Frank. Squeeze 'em as hard as you can."

I took hold of his hands. They were pale, beautifully manicured, deceptively slender. I could feel the pulse beating in his wrists as I took hold of him. I did as he asked and squeezed as hard as I could. I watched his face, but his expression never changed. If anything, the sharp glint in his eyes grew brighter and he grinned, showing his fine white teeth. "Take it easy, kid. You'll break my fingers!"

"I'm sorry." I dropped his hands and backed away. "I didn't mean to squeeze so hard."

He wrapped his hands around the back of my neck, cupped my jaw, and held me there. "How would you like to work for me, huh?" He shook me gently as he spoke, punctuating his question. "Think you'd like that, Frank? I need a doorman for my place up on West 34th street. You interested? Three hundred dollars a week to start, and then we'll see." He held my face, and for a moment, I had the strangest sensation he wanted to kiss me. Then stepping away, he took a small yellow card out of his wallet and handed it to me. "Tomorrow night, say seven? I'll meet you there. Give Cal your address, and I'll have my driver drop off a uniform."

NICKY'S nightclub was called The Dive, and even with my limited knowledge of the world, I figured this had to be ironic. The place was huge, a glistening silver dome spangled with tiny lights that blinked and sparkled overhead. At one end of the main ballroom, a huge stage reared above the dancers, and it was here that The Dive's dedicated orchestra, Boots Ramsay and His Bluebloods, played the latest tunes. The band members were all outfitted in white tuxedos with silver lamé lapels, and there were cigarette girls in silver stockings and tiny skirts, and cocktail waitresses whose costumes were the merest shimmer of silk, and impeccable waiters in dinner jackets and spotless white gloves. It was swank and then some. On Saturday nights Nick would make his appearance on the dance floor with his latest girl, and then he would retire to the bar to drink a cocktail and offer his regards to all the staff.

On my first night there, I heard one of the other doormen say Nick owned several dozen clubs around the city and made preordained stops at each one on its own particular night. Sometimes he'd arrive with a beautiful woman on his arm and leave with one of the cigarette girls or a cocktail waitress or a fashion model. He was always polite and courteous, and he was always flanked by two large young men who made it their business to plow through the crowd ahead of Nick and remove any potential obstacles. There was never any outright trouble of the sort you read about in newspapers, and in all the time I worked there, I never heard of anybody getting a snootful and shooting up the joint. There were always minor celebrities in attendance, and once, in our later acquaintance, Nick introduced me to a dark-haired young man whose name he said was Dillinger. I still don't know if that was true, and anyway, Dillinger kept most of his business in or near Chicago.

My job—as it was explained to me—was to stand in front of the nightclub's main entrance underneath the awning, "impeccable and handsome, kid," open the door for patrons coming or going, and flag down taxicabs as needed. A young Brooklyn Irish kid named

Mark Donnelly often parked his hack out front to wait for fares, and there were many of the slower nights I passed the time with him, listening to his car radio and smoking or taking a nip or three from the hip flask he carried. If it happened that we anticipated a bigger than usual crowd at The Dive, I would carefully monitor visitors and only admit the sorts of people Nicky deemed acceptable. If somebody got lippy or took it in his head to jump the line, I had Nicky's personal authority to shove him back, and I did. It got so that I almost wanted someone to try it on, just so I could throw my weight around.

A couple of months after I started working for him, we had a huge party at The Dive, with a lot of Nicky's personal friends and their women in attendance. Nick had ordered special uniforms for all his staff, each one individually tailored to fit like the proverbial glove. I never had a suit made just for me, had never been to a tailor in my life, and the only time I'd ever worn a tie—outside of working for Nick—was on the occasion of my First Holy Communion.

Nick himself supervised the fitting of my clothes, taking me to his personal tailor on 8th Avenue in the garment district. The fitting was something else. I'd never had another man's hands on me, and I wasn't sure what to do or where to look—and when the tailor asked me what side I dressed, I had no idea what he was talking about. Nick was kind; he didn't laugh at me. *He wants to know which side your tackle hangs, left or right.* And, when I still didn't know what he was talking about, Nick indicated the area in question on himself. *He needs to know which way your dick swings, kid. It's an honest question.*

Left, I guess, Mr. Brooks, sir. I never noticed.

Riding back to the club with Nick in the backseat of a cab was a novel experience as well. We sat close together, and as he talked, he would pick up my hand in his and squeeze it, smiling like we shared a private joke. His leg lay close beside mine, and he made no move to shift himself, even though the seat was large enough for us to sit at opposite ends of the cab if we'd wanted to. Now and then he'd move and his leg would rub against mine. I liked the way it felt. When the cabbie let us out in front of the club, Nick insisted I come into his private office, because he wanted to see how well the suit was going to fit and he had some other things for me to try on if I didn't mind. He closed and locked the door behind us and poured us both a hefty slug of whisky from the glass decanter on his desk.

"You did very well today, Frank. You did us both proud. You know how to act around people, the way to be if you want to be noticed and remembered." He lifted his glass to me. "I knew I was right to hire you. You've got everything a young man needs to get ahead in the world." He refilled our glasses and came around the desk to where I was standing. "Do you mind if I try something, Frank?"

"Like what?" My heart was pounding and the alcohol was going to my head. I felt like the room and everything around me was vaguely unreal, a spectacle enacted for my benefit.

"I like to be comfortable." He laid his glass down on the desk and reached for the knot of my tie. "You know? It's good to be comfortable." His face was less than a hand's breadth from mine, so close I could see each individual eyelash and each hair in his dark brows. "Do you want to be comfortable, Frank?"

"Yeah, sure." I wet my lips. "Sure, Nick. I like to be comfortable." I had no idea what was going on, and I didn't know if I should stay or bolt. Maybe he was trying some kind of Chinese angle to get me to come over to his side, which made no sense. Anybody with eyes could see I was already there.

"You really are the best of all my boys. You know that, huh?" He rested his hands on my shoulders. "The best of my boys." He caressed my cheek with the backs of his knuckles, and I couldn't help myself—I leaned into the gesture. "The best."

I closed my eyes and felt something hot and wet snake into my mouth, something I realized was his tongue. I wrapped my palm around the nape of his neck and pulled him to me and kissed him. I let him walk me backward to the sofa and lower me down gently. He undid my fly, pulled my shirt up, and took my cock out and sucked it into his mouth. In four or five strokes, I was coming, spending myself in hard, jagged bursts as my pleasure took me in its teeth and shook me.

"God. You're a hot one," he murmured. He wiped his mouth in a monogrammed handkerchief. "Couldn't wait, huh?"

I was too embarrassed to tell him this was my first time, so I mumbled some excuse about having to get home or my mother would worry. I dressed as quick as I could and got out of there.

When I came to work the next night, an envelope was stuck on my locker, with a note inside: "Have dinner with me." I didn't need to read the signature to know who it was from. I hid the note, and that night after work, I let Nicky Brooks take me to an exclusive midtown supper club and then to bed.

"I'm your boy, I guess." We lay together smoking in the dark, Nick and I, my body aching with the things he'd done. I suppose I was in love with him.

"You're my boy," Nick said. He leaned over and kissed me. "You can get dressed now. Just make sure you lock the door on your way out, huh? I'll see you later at the club."

He rolled over, his naked back to me, and that was it. I'd been dismissed. That was how I learned that, even though Nicky Brooks had taken me into his bed, he would never, ever take me into his heart.

"FRANKIE BOY, is that you?" The voice on the other end was unmistakable.

"Yeah, it's me."

"Do you know who this is? Go on, then, guess."

In a city full of Irish accents, I had no trouble picking out Eamonn Molloy's. "Eamonn—or should I say, Chief—it's good to hear from you." It was very late, well past midnight, but I was relieved to hear from him. I hadn't been here very long, but some nights the walls of my place felt like they were closing in on me.

"Nah, never mind that Chief nonsense. I was wondering if you'd mind coming round to see me."

"Now?"

"Weren't in bed, were you?"

"No, I was just sitting here having a drink."

"You can come over here and have a drink, can't you?" He chuckled. "I've got a bottle of some very nice Irish here."

"I'll be there. At your place?" It occurred to me I didn't actually know where he lived.

"Nah, come over to the cop shop. I'm working late. Bring nothing but your own sweet self."

The hum of the dial tone filled my ear. I didn't hesitate. I called a taxi, and within five minutes, I was standing in Eamonn's office at Fort Townsend. The constabulary headquarters were nowhere near the level of busyness I'd have expected from a police station on a Friday night, but I reminded myself this wasn't New York. Apart from the occasional soldier or seaman on a bender, there were few occurrences requiring police intervention.

Eamonn was sitting at his desk, his face illuminated by the small circle of light cast by a tiny lamp; a pile of papers in front of him testified to his onerous work load. "Ah, Frankie boy, there you are, thanks be to Jesus." He shoved some papers out of his way and stood up, hand extended to greet me. "Did I frighten you at all? I honest to God lost track of the time." He moved past me to close— and lock—the office door. "Don't mind me. I'm that addled, I don't know if I'm punched, bored, or shot out of a gun. Give us a hug, will ya?"

He hauled me into his arms, and I clutched him, pressing my body into his. He smelled of tobacco smoke and fine wool cloth and aftershave lotion. I cupped his face between my palms and kissed him, drowning in the heat of him, the feel and taste and smell.

"We're in the middle of a recruiting drive," he said, when we broke apart, "if you can believe that. Do you know what the war's done to the ranks of able-bodied young men around here? Not to mention the half dozen or so with a particle of common sense. It's criminal." He sat down again in the small circle of light, and I followed, moving to stand behind him.

"Eamonn." I slid my palms down his shoulders, smoothing his chest. "Why not leave this for later, hm?" I hesitated to add I was so horny I could have barked. "Maybe I can make you forget about it." His shirt was unbuttoned at the front, and I slipped my hand inside, stroking a nipple to hardness.

"Mm—Frankie—don't be at that." He sighed. "God forgive me, you're enough to put a man out of his wits." He slid a sheet of paper into the light. "I've been on the wire all night long, trying to get in touch with New York. We put out a general recruitment call to some of the NYPD precincts, and I'm glad to say we've had a few replies. Some are on their way here even as we speak."

"New York, huh?" My hand moved to his other nipple, teasing, touching. His rigid cock was making a tent of his trousers. "Well, that's nice." I kissed the side of his neck. "I think we should pick up where we left off, Eamonn."

"How is your investigation going?" he asked with a catch in his throat.

I leaned over far enough to touch his cock. "The Roarkes are all crazy. In fact, I think this whole goddamn town is crazy." I moved around to the front, pushed his chair back a ways, knelt down, and laid my mouth over the bulge in his pants.

"Ah." His fingers tangled in my hair. "Jesus."

"But you know, Eamonn…." I undid his fly, delved inside, and freed his cock from the confines of his shorts. "I'm very tenacious." His cock was full, flushed a deep, rosy red, and the head was slicked with his body's covert moisture. "Tell me to stay away from something and I never listen." I licked him, and he hissed through his teeth, his grip tightening on my scalp. "Give me an inch—" I sucked the head into my mouth and worked it gently before letting it go. "—and I'll take the whole nine yards."

He trembled as I took him deep into my mouth and pleasured him, varying the speed and pressure, repeatedly bringing him close to his release and then backing off until he was nearly weeping, begging me to let him come. "Frankie, for the love of Jesus, oh, for the love of God—" He arched his back and went silent, still, and rigid, every muscle drawn taut as a bowstring. His face flushed and his lips were drawn back in an ecstatic rictus. "Jesus." He exhaled violently and his body sagged back into the chair. I sat back on my heels and fumbled for my handkerchief to wipe my mouth. "Frankie." He pulled me to him and kissed me, and I returned it eagerly. I took his hand and laid it on my cock, wanting him and unwilling to wait any longer. "Not here." He pushed me away gently. "Look, you go on back to your place and I'll come there." He drew me to my feet and kissed me again. "You go on home, and as soon as I'm finished here, I'll come to you."

His attitude confused me. "Eamonn, you called me—"

"Yes, I know that, and I swear to you, I'll be over to yours in a minute. Hand on heart, Frankie."

Before I knew what was happening I'd been shut out into the corridor, my hat in my hand. The clock at the end of the hall read 12:47 a.m.

I caught a taxi home and waited in my apartment until three thirty, when I finally fell asleep. I dreamed I was standing on a high parapet, alone, while fierce winds howled around me and the sky grew black with storm clouds. I could hear someone calling to me in the distance, someone whose voice I recognized, but when I tried to shout a greeting, I found I was absolutely voiceless.

Chapter Five

MY INVESTIGATION of the Roarke insurance case had led me down one blind alley after another. The resolution of the claim had dragged on now for weeks, and my boss was beginning to lose his patience. I'd gone in to see him that morning to present my expense account claim and to advise him of my progress.

"You know, Boyle, you came highly recommended, but I'm beginning to wonder if your friend from the 40th Precinct wasn't selling me a pig in a poke." He peered up at me through the thick lenses of his black, horn-rimmed glasses. "You've been on this case for weeks, and so far you've turned up nothing of any use. The woman is dead, and as far as that goes, we're liable for the claim, which means we have to pay up one way or the other." He shook his head. "This nonsense about fraud and the crazy sister—not to mention several dubious leads related to indecent artwork—makes me wonder if you even know your business at all."

I sank onto the chair beside his desk. "Mr. Koestler, you've been real good to me ever since I got here, and I don't want to let you down." I picked up a snow globe and shook it, watching the tiny white flakes settle on the miniature town inside. "I've been an investigator for a long time, long enough to trust my instincts when it comes to things like this." Things like what? A family hell-bent on their own self-destruction? A seriously melancholic mother who had probably—but not absolutely—thrown herself off a four-hundred-foot cliff into the icy North Atlantic? A hypothesis of insurance fraud I was nowhere near to proving? I could kind of see his point. "There's something not right about this. There are a lot of things that aren't right."

He harrumphed loudly as he lit his pipe. "Your instincts are of no use unless they uncover something." He shook out the spent match and tossed it into an ashtray. "You say you don't think this Roarke woman is dead. Can you prove it?"

"Mr. Koestler, I—" Christ, did he think I could work miracles?

"If she's not dead, where is she?" He puffed on his pipe, filling the air with the scent of expensive tobacco. "Hiding under the wharf? Hauling fish off the Grand Banks?" He leaned forward and fixed me with a gimlet stare. "Let me guess: she's hiding in a secret room somewhere in her own house."

"I need more time… a week, two weeks. It's not enough." I tossed my expense sheets onto his desk. "Here. Honor these, or don't, it doesn't matter."

"Boyle! What the devil is the matter with you? Are you sick or something?"

"Never felt better in my life." I tossed him my biggest, brightest smile. "Don't go anywhere. If I'm right—and I think I am—then this whole case is ready to bust wide open."

I WALKED into the Heartache just after noon. The sun was shining and the air had that pleasant chill you associate with autumn. I'd slept well and I felt real good. I went in and took my usual seat at the bar. I'd spent the morning at City Hall, poring over the blueprints of the Roarke house that some enterprising lawyer had thoughtfully appended to the mortgage rolls, which were, of course, viewable by the public. The house was one of the oldest in the city, dating back to the 19th century. It had been built the same time as many of the gracious old Queen Anne-style mansions on Circular

Road and Rennies Mill and had luckily been spared the ravages of the two major fires that had all but destroyed the city.

The entrance to the Roarke house was through a main door at the front, opening into a larger foyer, which let into a crawing room. The house had the usual number of bedrooms for the era, as well as servants' quarters, a summer kitchen, and an attic. Under the main staircase, there was the usual empty space, which most people used for storage, but not the Roarkes. The draftsman had drawn stairs where a rudimentary closet ought to have gone—drawn it in the dashed lines used on blueprints to indicate a hidden object.

Hidden stairs *under* the stairs? Why? More to the point, where did the stairs go? I'd heard about some of the older houses downtown, how there were secret tunnels leading to the waterfront, and of course, there was Mr. Temple's story about the hidden room. Was the Roarke house similarly equipped? If Mr. Temple was telling the truth—and I had no reason to believe he wasn't—it was definitely hiding more than the usual closet-bound skeletons.

"You look like a man who's discovered the secrets of the universe." Jack laid a fresh cup of coffee in front of me. "Care to share the wealth?"

"Oh, it's just business." I poured sugar into my coffee and stirred it. "Good news, I guess you could say. I finally busted something free, after all this time."

"I see." He pulled a pad from his apron pocket. "Soup and sandwich for you?"

"Sure, you know, the usual." I'd taken a liking to Jack's split pea soup, and his roast beef on white could have given many a New York deli a run for its money.

"You're a creature of habit, Frank." Jack tore off the order and tacked it up with the rest. "We're kind of busy, so it might take a few minutes longer. That okay with you?"

"Sure." I glanced around; the place was packed. "Business seems to be good."

"It is." Jack gazed at the crowd. "We get our share of the locals, but mostly it's Americans who frequent my place. I guess it reminds them of home." He sighed, and there was something wistful in it.

"You ever get homesick?" I asked.

"Sure," he said. "Doesn't everybody?"

I didn't want to say it, but Jack's homesickness hung on him like an invisible overcoat, and when he spoke, there was a palpable loneliness in his voice. "Sometimes." I sipped my coffee. "Sometimes a change is as good as a rest. How long you been here?"

"Oh, just before the war, thereabouts." He laughed. "Sometimes I don't even remember."

"You're from Philly, aren't you?" A woman sitting near the back of the café laughed, a deep belly laugh. My mother used to laugh like that.

"How can you tell?" He kept his eyes on the bar, but I knew what I'd said had hit a nerve.

"Your accent, for one." I shrugged. "I've been all over the place, myself." I lit a cigarette while I waited for my meal. "Maybe we can have a couple of drinks one of these days, talk about home?"

He shook his head. "I never use it. Coffee, on the other hand—"

A voice from behind Jack spoke his name in an accent I'd never heard before. The owner of the voice stepped out from the back room. "Jack, I'm going now, but I'll be back in an hour or two, no more." He was perhaps five feet nine inches tall, fit and spare, with the intimation of great power in his slender body. He was beautiful—handsome was too weak a word—with huge, liquid, dark eyes and a lean, intelligent face. His mouth under a tightly groomed mustache was beautifully shaped and his expression pleasantly curious. He extended his hand. "Samuel Halim, Cairo Police Department. I'm afraid we haven't met, but Jack has told me much about you."

"Pleased to meet you." I shook his hand; his grip was firm, cool, and strong. I had the impression he could kick my ass six ways to Sunday if he wanted to. "You must find it cold in these parts." What the hell was a Cairo cop doing in Newfoundland?

"It's true, the climate could do to be a fair bit warmer, but I'm not here for the weather." He smiled, and my gut did a little flip-flop. He was the sexiest goddamn thing I'd ever seen. "But now I must take my leave of you. Jack? Dinner this evening?"

"Sure thing, Sam, *Inshallah.*" He affected nonchalance, but his gaze as he looked at Halim was hungry, like a man who was desperately in love. I thought I knew why he wasn't serving overseas, why he hadn't joined up after Pearl Harbor, but I didn't want to be the one to say it. Or maybe he'd already been in, and they'd kicked him out on a blue ticket....

"I've got a Sam myself," I said. "Kind of."

"He's in the insurance racket too?"

I grinned. "No, he's a cop... somebody I knew, back in the Bronx." Just then my lunch arrived. Jack went off to do some work in his office, and I was alone at the bar with the daily paper and the hum and bustle of people all around me. The news was about what I'd expect: advertisements for everything from stove piping—"in view of the difficulty in obtaining, etc."—to cotton blankets to women's woolen hose, government notices about the necessity of saving one's scrap rubber, and advice on how to properly use Dr. Thomas's Eclectric Oil to ease the pain of rheumatism. The news—heavily censored—featured reports from the front exulting how well the war was going for Our Side and featuring grainy photographs of "Hitlerites" surrendering to the Red Army on the Kharkov Front.

"...sure she'll put out, just as long as I keep the silk stockings coming. I tell ya, I've got her eating out of my hand. And you know where my hand's been!"

The voice was unfamiliar, but likely belonged to one of three American soldiers sitting in the booth directly abutting my end of the bar. They were young, maybe twenty, clean shaven, and nice looking, and probably headed for an ignominious death somewhere in the blood-soaked fighting fields of Africa or Europe.

"Yeah, but sweet Jesus, Lloyd, ain't you afraid you're gonna get caught? You know what they'll do to you." The second voice was unmistakably Southern and slightly older. By turning my head just a fraction of an inch, I saw him: burly, big through the chest and shoulders, and with the beginnings of a paunch. "There's enough of that going on around here."

"Yeah, and I'm gonna get my share," the first one said.

Understand that I'm not naive. I figured local women, like women everywhere, wanted nice things and were more likely to go with men who could provide them with certain consumer goods, but what these boys were doing—if they were doing it and not just talking about it—could get them into a whole heap of trouble.

"Say, what's the black market like around here?" I asked Jack as I paid my lunch check.

He raised his eyebrows. "You think I'd know the answer to that question?"

I laughed. "Not you."

"Well, good." He affected an expression of hurt as he tossed me my change. "Thought I'd have to duel you for my reputation there, friend." He shrugged. "I guess we got much the same thing here that goes on anywhere else. Silk stockings, chocolate, booze, you name it. The cops try to crack down on it, but they can't be everywhere. A lot of these gangster types from the States caught wind of what was going on here and followed the band, so to speak. Unfortunately for the local people, we're building more than just bases up here."

I handed him a sizeable tip. "Thanks, Jack."

"For lunch?"

"For everything. I'll hit you up later in the week. We'll have a poker night, huh?"

"You got it."

I reached to take my hat off the rack when the sound of screaming sirens stopped me cold. A police car hurled down the street, then another, followed by an ambulance. Some of the café's customers ran outside to see what was happening, while others lined the plate glass windows, eager for the best view. I shouldered my way through the crowd to where a late-model roadster lay slewed across the streetcar tracks in the middle of the road.

I got as close as I could before one of the attending policemen—Alphonsus Picco—put out his hand and stopped me. "You'll need to keep back, sir. We've got to let the ambulance men get at her." He saw who I was. "Frank Boyle."

"Hi, Sergeant." I nodded toward the car. "Road accident?"

"Not exactly." He grimaced. "This is one of the worst ones I've ever seen."

"I seen it, Constable!" A skinny boy, maybe fourteen years old, squeezed his way through the crowd and hung on Picco's elbow. "She was driving down the road with some fellow in the car. He jumped out and ran away." He pointed toward the harbor. "That way. Probably got on a boat or something."

"I seen him too," someone else shouted. The crowd bucked and swayed dangerously, and Picco shouted to three constables standing nearby to keep them back. "She was driving and talking to that man." A large woman, carrying a string bag of onions and a dead codfish, pushed her way to the front of the group. "He was skinny in the face and kind of dark. They stopped when the signal turned, and I heard a bang."

"Keep back, the crowd of ye!" Picco shoved at a young man who was elbowing him in the side. "I'll take the whole Jesus crowd of ye in, if ye don't stop!" He stumbled back against me. "You picked a great time to show up, Boyle."

Picco's admonition worked, and everyone pulled back, crowding onto the sidewalk and murmuring among themselves. I had a clear line of sight to the accident, and it wasn't pretty. Her killer had knotted a silk stocking around her pale throat and tied it in a bow. There were no ligature marks on her dewy skin, and looking at her face, I knew why. The stocking hadn't killed her. The bullet hole in the middle of her forehead had done the trick. "Jesus."

The dead woman in the car was Felice Roarke.

A plainclothes detective was on his knees beside the car, combing the ground for the spent casing. As I came near, he got up, dusted his hands together, and passed a small, brown paper bag to one of the uniformed cops. He was about my height, lean, and slender; he wore a tan trench coat belted around his middle and a dark fedora tilted on one side, but there was no mistaking him. The detective in question was Sam Lipinski.

Chapter Six

"TELL me how this is possible." Sam and I sat at a corner table in the Heartache. I couldn't stop looking at him. "The last thing I know, you're putting me on a plane to this godforsaken place, and now, here you are." I reached under the table and squeezed the arm closest to me. "Goddammit, Sam, what the hell is going on?"

He looked grim, thinner than when I'd last seen him, and he'd cut himself shaving: there was a tiny nick near the corner of his mouth, a miniscule wound I ached to kiss. There were dark circles under his eyes, and he was smoking much more than he usually did. "I won't lie to you, Frank. I been through hell these past couple months." He toyed with his coffee cup, turning it around and around in the saucer, his gaze faraway. "Everything went to hell after you left." He caught my look and hastily amended this. "Nothing to do with you. Precinct stuff." He laughed mirthlessly. "Cop stuff."

"What kind of cop stuff?"

He shook his head. "Nothing good." Reaching into his pocket, he took out a silver tube, uncapped one end, and put it in his mouth, inhaling sharply. "Few days after you left, one of our guys, Mick Curran, organized a raid on one of Nicky Brooks's clubs—The Dive, I think it's called—pretty swank place." He took a sip of his coffee; his hands were trembling. "Dunno what happened, but they were tipped off. Couple of my guys got shot up pretty badly, and I lost young Jimmy Dolan. He'd only been on the force for a year."

"Jesus, Sam, I'm sorry."

"When Nicky Brooks came back from Sing Sing, he came all the way back. Worst part of it was, he'd been making friends and influencing people, you might say."

"What do you mean?"

He sighed. "On the force. Not just our precinct. It was pretty much city wide. He managed to corrupt or otherwise compromise a whole lotta cops, some you'd never even suspect. I caught wind of it and decided to do a little bit of investigating on my own time."

"I can just imagine how that turned out."

"Yeah." He uncapped the inhaler and took another puff. "Couple weeks ago I got a private, personal message delivered to my apartment. A paper bag full of dog shit. That, along with a few other things, made me think I'd be better off somewhere else." He pulled a scrap of paper out of his wallet and tossed it onto the table. "Nice economy of words, but I found the sentiment a bit wanting."

I unfolded it. It was a crude note, written on cheap newsprint with a thick black pencil: "Keep your big kike nose out of it." I winced. "Nice."

"That's not all. I been in the hospital."

Sam had come out of the precinct building one night after working late and found four guys—fellow police officers—waiting for him. He shouted for help, but the rest of the building was, as he put it, "strangely deaf." By the time his assailants had finished with him, he had three broken ribs, a broken collarbone, a busted nose, two black eyes, and various internal injuries. "Kind of a hard way to take a vacation, if you know what I mean."

I felt a dangerous heat suffuse my face. "Those sons of bitches! I oughta—"

He laid a gentle hand on my arm. "It's done, Frankie. Don't worry about it. Few weeks flat on my back, and I'm almost as good as new." He smiled. "God, I missed you."

"I missed you, too, Sam." I wondered when I'd get around to telling him about Eamonn Molloy. It wasn't the sort of topic you'd breach in casual conversation. *Hey Sam, I met this Irishman. We get together and suck each other off.* No, it wasn't the sort of thing I could ever talk to him about, and it wasn't just because Sam was such a straight arrow, in a manner of speaking.

I had met Sam Lipinski several years before at his father's butcher shop in the Bronx, not too far from where I was living at the time. He and I were contemporaries, but he'd gone to a different high school and our relationship didn't go much beyond a nodding acquaintance. Besides, I ran with a rougher crowd, the local toughs who hung out on the front stoops of each other's houses and hooted catcalls at the girls as they went by, or tossed rotten apples at the beat cops, or raced each other to the streetcar that passed at regular intervals. I wasn't one for studying or staying after school to make up what I'd missed. I often cut my afternoon classes to shoot pool with Benny Phinster and Joe and some of the boys down at Lou Pinelli's lounge on the corner of Grant and East 166th.

Sam was the overly studious son of my old lady's Jewish butcher. When he wasn't studying, he was taking dancing lessons, or singing lessons, or catching the subway uptown to try out for some play, and I'd hear how he got a part in a show, dancing and singing, but it was never anything anybody in our neighborhood cared about. He didn't shoot pool with the rest of the guys or play stickball in the vacant lot behind Mrs. Temmolini's fruit store, and he didn't hang out on the stoop talking dirty about some neighborhood jane. He was a real straight arrow.

I'd been on the West Coast for a few years, ever since that business with my brother Leo, and I guess I didn't have too much to come back here for. I'd ended up apprenticed—for lack of a better word—to Charlie Blackwell, an alcoholic private dick operating out of Los Angeles. He was a world-weary man who lived on booze and cigarette smoke and whose clientele was mostly made up of various down-and-outers, people for whom he was the absolute last hope. He handled the kind of dirty cases nobody else would touch—nasty divorces, typically—and kept a minor harem of girls on retainer, ready to jump into bed and be photographed with some poor bastard, all at a moment's notice. But he was decent to me, and he taught me the business, and in our off hours, he showed me he could just about suck a golf ball through fifty feet of garden hose and then some. By the time I came back East, I had enough know-how and experience to set up my own agency, which is what I did. I started out doing the usual stuff—surveillance, wiretaps, now and then putting a tail on a guy—but eventually I graduated to insurance work, which paid a lot better than the other stuff.

Truth be told, I hadn't even thought about Sam Lipinski in all the years I'd been gone. He was just a skinny Jewish kid who spent all his time reading *Playbill* and learning show tunes, just the local butcher's son. It was a warm day in early June when I ended up in Dutch Lipinski's shop, looking for my sister. The back door of Lipinski's shop opened and a dapper young man stepped through. The last person I thought he'd be was Sam. Not this guy. He was as tall as me, broad-shouldered, lean and athletic, with a dancer's flat belly and easy grace. He was beautifully and expensively dressed in a dark-gray suit and his curly black hair had been tamed and combed to one side, revealing a high forehead and piercing dark eyes. A tightly groomed mustache partly covered his upper lip, but apart from that, he was clean-shaven. Seeing him was like being run down by a bus. I'm serious. I went hot and cold all over, and something way down deep inside of me began to throb with a discrete pulse of its own. I was suddenly wondering what it might be like to hold him naked next to me and kiss his perfect mouth.

"Oh, Frankie," Dutch motioned me over. "You know my son, Sam? I think you two might have gone to school together. Sam's a police officer. He just made detective, didn't you, Sam?"

"Frank Boyle," I said, shaking his hand. "You probably don't remember me."

"Sure I do." He grinned, but there was a gentle mockery in it. "You used to hang out on Mrs. Grammer's stoop, you and all the other guys. Whatcha been up to? Still talking trash?"

He invited me to go for a drink, so I did. It was awkward at first, because I couldn't reconcile the way he looked now with the skinny kid who spent all his time at lessons. We ended up in Vito's

Bar, a little hole-in-the-wall place around the corner from the tenement where I grew up. Vito's was as dark as the ace of spades even in full daylight, with maybe a dozen tables scattered around a space the size of your average suburban garage. Vito himself was somewhere between fifty and dead, with a bulging belly and skin as yellow as old parchment. He had a habit of lighting a cigarette and letting it hang out of the corner of his mouth so the ashes dropped on whatever surface he happened to be standing over.

Sam and I took a table near the back. He pulled out a silver cigarette case and offered me one, and I struck a match and lit for both of us. "How long's it been, Frankie? Jeez, you left for the coast right about the time Leo—" Even in that darkness, he must have seen the expression on my face, because he stopped talking and changed the subject. "Long time, huh?"

"Yeah. After Leo…." I took several quick sips of my drink to cover. "I figured the best thing for me to do was to go away for a while, you know?"

"That bad?" His hand lay on the table between us, the fingernails clean and beautifully manicured. He wore a pinkie ring, some kind of signet with a small diamond in the corner.

My gut clenched. "He was nothing to Nicky Brooks and his guys. Nothing. Less than nothing. They treated him like he was just a dog in the street, like garbage. They didn't even care." The old, familiar ache started up behind my eyes, and I'll be damned if I didn't almost start bawling. It took me a few minutes to get myself under control, but Sam didn't say a word. He had a way of sitting with you that made you feel it was okay to just keep quiet, that he would wait 'til you were ready to speak again. "But that's old news. And you, what's up with this cop routine of yours, huh?" I took a fold of his lapel between thumb and finger and rubbed the fine cloth. "I'd have laid odds on you becoming a rabbi or something, maybe a Broadway hoofer uptown."

He laughed, a wonderful laugh that creased the smooth skin of his face in interesting ways. I liked looking at him. "Me, a rabbi?

Yeah, *shalom aleichem* to you too. You're funny, Frank. I guess me being a rabbi is about as likely as you being a priest, huh?"

"No way. I still remember Brother Mike telling us in sixth grade about how fornication was a mortal sin. He rounded us all up and put the fear of God into us." Remembering it now, I started to laugh, but it hadn't been so funny back when. "Scared the hell out of me. I was terrified to even touch my pecker. It made taking a piss a whole lot more complicated, I can tell you that."

He downed the rest of his drink and signaled Vito for another. "So celibacy wasn't an option for you." His dark eyes took me in, and I'm not flattering myself when I say there was open admiration there. He liked what he saw.

"Nope." I couldn't help myself; I broke out laughing. "Some things you don't mess with."

"Good." He quickly sobered. "I'm glad you reconsidered that decision, Frank." His hand still lay on the table between us, and he reached out, stroking the side of my hand with the very tip of his thumb. "I'm real glad."

My cock twitched and I was glad of the dark, because I knew my cheeks were burning just then. "I thought maybe you'd end up on the stage," I said, just to change the subject. "You took all those lessons when we were kids. What happened?"

He didn't answer for a minute or two, and I thought maybe I'd screwed up. When he finally spoke, his voice had lost its sensual edge and he merely sounded sad. "It's no career, Frank. Not for a boy like me." He gazed into his glass, turning it around and around. "I guess I figured if I tried hard enough, you know? Learned my trade… maybe I'd get a break."

I reached out and laid my hand on the back of his wrist, but only for a minute. "It didn't work out?"

"My old man said that only queers were interested in singing and dancing onstage—if I made my career that way, everybody would think I was a homosexual. My mother was the one who sent me for lessons. I guess maybe she had dreams for me. My old man, he didn't care what I did back then, as long as I kept out of his way. You know how it is." He took a sip of his drink. "When I told him I wanted to be on Broadway, he blew his top. It was okay for after school when I was just a kid, but not now. A grown man, dancing and singing? He said he didn't want the neighborhood thinking I was a queer, and if I wanted to sing so bad, I could be a cantor. Yeah, he made a real big thing about it."

"Jesus."

"I told him there was no way I was being a cantor. So the next day, I went down and joined the force." He grinned. "In twenty years I'll retire with a full pension. You can't argue with that."

No, I thought, *you can't argue with that, as long as you live to collect that pension.* The idea of Sam being gunned down in the line of duty was always a possibility. It was dangerous, dirty work he was doing. I wanted to say something, to tell him to be careful, but the words wouldn't come. I figured maybe I didn't have the right. In the end I didn't say anything at all. We spent maybe three hours drinking and talking before Sam looked at his watch and said he was supposed to be on duty in an hour. We walked back the way we'd come and said good-bye in front of my apartment house and that was it.

I didn't see him for maybe another eight or nine months, right after Nicky Brooks got out of Sing Sing, sprung by the efforts of a singularly slimy lawyer. He told anyone who'd listen he was coming after me. It was my testimony, after all, that had gotten him sent upstate in the first place. What happened to Leo was Nicky's fault, 100 percent. He knew it and I knew it, and when it came time to testify against him, I was there, front and center. The last thing Nicky said before they took him away was *I'll get you, Boyle. Just you wait. There's nowhere you can hide from me.*

"SO NOW I'm here. I answered a recruitment call—figured it was time to get the hell out of there." He rolled the inhaler between his fingers. "I didn't want to go, but what could I do? It got really ugly.

Coupla guys even came to see me in the hospital, paid their respects." He dropped his voice. "But what kind of a place this is, huh? A person's gotta have some *chutzpah* to live here, am I right?"

I couldn't help myself. I reached across and squeezed his hand. "So what about Nicky Brooks?"

He lit a cigarette. "Nicky Brooks is, as far as I know, still alive and well in New York City. He's fallen on tough times, you know." He shook out the match and dropped it in the ashtray. "Just after you left, the Spinelli brothers decided they wanted a piece of Nicky's action. It ended up in a pretty nasty showdown, and a few of Nicky's places got firebombed. He went across the river to have it out with Bruno Spinelli, but Bruno took exception to it, and him and his boys ran Nicky off. Last I heard he was gone to ground somewhere, nobody knows."

"Maybe he came here." I laughed, but it wasn't funny.

"Hard to say." He rolled the tip of his cigarette around the rim of the ashtray. "Does he even know this place exists? Maybe. I don't know him as well as you do."

I was sure he meant nothing by it. All the same, there was something in his tone I hadn't heard before—something angry and possibly dangerous. "I—we—Christ, Sam, I worked for him when I was a kid, but that was a long time ago."

"You don't need to explain anything to me, Frankie." He looked at his watch. "I gotta get back to headquarters. I need to go over some stuff with Picco." He stood up and buttoned his coat. "You know, he's a pretty smart cop."

"Sam, who killed the Roarke girl?" The bullet hole was par for the course, but the silk stocking really threw me for a loop.

His expression was sardonic, familiarly so. It made a little pain in my chest. "I thought maybe you could tell me."

THE next morning I caught the streetcar up to Royle's Flowers and bought the most luxurious funeral bouquet my expense account could bear. I wasn't sure which blooms the late Felice Roarke would have favored, so I instructed the girl to make me up a bunch of whatever they had. Then I hailed a taxi and rode up Duckworth Street, past the Newfoundland Hotel, and down Kings Bridge Road to the Roarke house. The windows were shuttered and a black mourning wreath was hung on the door, and I made my footsteps as quiet as possible on the cement walk.

It took several raps at the knocker before Vivian Roarke arrived to answer the door. She was wearing a black crepe-de-chine morning dress, and her hair was gathered into a knot at the back of her neck. Her pale face was completely bare of makeup. "Mr. Boyle. How did I know you'd be the first to turn up?" She stepped back to allow me entry into the house. "Is this a social call, or are you here to determine whether my sister is quite dead as well?"

I handed her the flowers. "I didn't know which flowers Felice might have preferred. I'm so sorry."

She examined the bouquet as if it might contain vermin before handing it off to a silent maid who appeared from the shadows. "So this is a social call."

"It is." I held out my hand. "You have my most profound sympathies."

She took my hand but only for a moment, turning away to dab at her eyes with a handkerchief. "You seem like the sort of man who takes death in his stride."

"I don't know if anyone ever learns to do that." I had a mental image of my brother Leo standing helpless in front of the drugstore where he was gunned down. He was seven years old. I could never forget the look on his face, right before the bullets hit him, right before he saw me, riding in the car. *Frankie!* I shook my head, willing away the memory.

"Please—sit down. Make yourself comfortable."

I followed her into the living room, a space full of gloom and dust motes. The sofa and chairs were covered in dark fabric, and the windows had been tightly shuttered. I noticed, too, that pictures had been turned to the wall and all the mirrors in the house were draped. This was a custom I'd seldom seen outside of Appalachia, or among those few Italian families who still kept to the old ways.

Vivian Roarke couldn't seem to settle herself, which didn't surprise me. Like her late sister, she had an overabundance of nervous energy, which expressed itself in a near-constant fidgeting. She adjusted her collar, the cuffs of her dress, and lit a cigarette, which she promptly put out again in the ashtray. Twice she got up and went to the shuttered windows to peer out at Kings Bridge Road before turning and stalking the length of the room. "I have something to ask you, Mr. Boyle, and it might seem like a strange question."

"By all means, let's have it." I lit a cigarette of my own and took a few sharp drags. Just looking at her was making me uneasy. "Anything to help you settle your nerves."

She stopped in front of me and stood with her skinny legs apart, the way a man does when he's aching to take that first swing. "Was it you, Mr. Boyle?"

For a minute or two, I didn't have a sweet clue what she was talking about. "Was *what* me?"

Her torso jerked back, as if I'd physically struck her. "You know what I mean."

I stubbed my cigarette out. "No, I don't think I do, but something tells me I'm not going to like it." A haze of blue smoke hung in the still air, a palpable cloud being slowly drawn away by some unseen vacuum just above and to the right of me. All these old houses were the same: palatial and grand on the outside, but drafty as all hell inside.

She clenched her fists, her arm muscles rigid. "Did you kill my sister?"

It was the sort of question you never expect to hear, but once you do, you can't get it out of your head. It's like a bad taste in your mouth, something you ate on a dare or while you were drunk off your ass, a lingering aversion nothing takes away. "Did I *what*?"

"Did you—" Her voice broke, but she kept on. "Did you kill Felice?"

"I dunno," I shot back. "Were you the one who sapped me down on Duckworth Street the other day? I woke up in McMurdo's Lane."

"Oh, don't be ridiculous!"

"Or maybe your good friend Dr. Nichol did it—a little message from you, perhaps? You'd better tell him to ease up. He's liable to kill somebody one of these days."

"Dr. Nichol is no friend of mine." She started a quick, jerky walk around the living room, her figure all sharp angles and broken glass. She stopped in front of me, swaying slightly, her face an unreadable blank.

"Really? He's got a pretty picture of your little sister in his private office. Kind of a cheesecake pose, if you know what I mean."

Her hand was a blur, the slap so hard it rocked me back on my heels.

"I think I'd better be going now." I picked up my hat and started for the door.

"Don't you go anywhere!" She got her hands around my arm and dug in, her sharp nails biting into the muscle. "You stay here until you answer me! Did you kill my sister? Did you?"

"Vivian, you need to see a doctor." What kind of doctor, I didn't say. I figured she could puzzle that one out for herself. "I'm genuinely sorry for your loss."

Maybe it was the way I said it, the tone of voice I used, or the way my face looked. I'll never be sure. Before I had a chance to turn away, she was on me, swearing, scratching, clawing for my eyes. I threw my arms up to try and protect my face, but it was no use. Her sharp nails scored several deep channels into my skin before she was pulled off of me.

"Vivian!" Mr. Roarke caught his daughter around the waist and pushed her down onto the sofa. "Stop this!"

"He killed Felice!" she cried. She pushed her father away and stood up.

"He did no such thing." Mr. Roarke handed her off to a servant, who bundled the still-sobbing Vivian into the kitchen. "Mr. Boyle, you must look over my daughter. She isn't herself. This… latest event is affecting us all."

I'd managed to stem the flow of blood with my handkerchief, but the scratches on my face hurt like a son of a bitch. "I came to pay my respects." I got the hint. "Please accept my condolences, Mr. Roarke. Felice's death is a real tragedy." I crammed my hat down on my head and got the hell out of there.

IT COST me $12 even to get my torn skin stitched back up at Grace General Hospital on LeMarchant Road and another $2.75 for a prescription ointment to combat any traces of infection Vivian's fingernails had left behind. The doc who stitched me up delivered a real nice lecture about wartime shortages and how it was just too bad young men couldn't appropriately restrain themselves. Didn't I know medication was a precious commodity these days?

I thanked him for his concern, paid for the ointment, and caught the streetcar back to my apartment.

I'D JUST gotten in when there was a knock at my apartment door. I lived over a dress shop on Water Street and my apartment, while hardly palatial, was well suited to my needs. It had a comfortable bedroom, full of gorgeous, antique wooden furniture, a modern kitchen, and a bathroom with a sinfully deep tub as well as a shower. Wartime water restrictions being what they were, I usually limited myself to a quick shower, but I looked forward to a long, hot soak someday soon.

The knocking intensified and it sounded pretty important, so I yanked the door open double-quick, expecting to see yet another pissed-off member of the Roarke family standing in the hall. Instead, Alphonsus Picco was at the door with Sam Lipinski, and they both looked pretty grim.

"How's it going, Frank?" Sam was unshaven and dark circles had appeared under his eyes. Both he and Picco found it necessary to show me their badges. "Mind if we ask you a few questions?"

"So this isn't a social call." I showed them into the kitchen. "Can I fetch you gents a drink?"

"We're on duty," Sam said. "Maybe another time." He was careful not to look at me.

Picco pointed past me at something on the table. His entire body was ramrod stiff. "Get your hands in the air and step away from the table, right now."

I stared at him like he'd sprouted horns. "What? What the hell are you talking about?"

Picco grabbed my shoulder, spun me around, and pinned me against the wall, my left arm twisted painfully behind me. Out of the corner of my eye, I saw him pick something up from my kitchen table: a revolver. Call me crazy, but it definitely hadn't been there that morning when I'd left for work, and I knew damn well it wasn't mine.

He handed it to Sam, who snapped open the chamber, sniffed, and snapped it shut again. "It's been fired."

"That's it, then," Picco said. I felt him fumbling around and then something cold and metallic snapped shut around my wrists. The bastard was handcuffing me.

"What the hell is this?" I turned my head, trying to see Sam, but he was occupied with the gun. "That isn't my gun. Goddammit, listen to me!"

"I'm going to have to take you in, Frank. I'm sorry. I'd question you here, but it wouldn't be official." Sam nodded to Picco. "Watch it on those stairs."

The ride to the lockup was mostly silent. I tried on several occasions to get Sam to tell me what the hell was going on, but he wouldn't even look at me. He and Picco conversed quietly in the front of the squad car while I sat by myself in the back seat. I carried a gun, sure; most private dicks had one, for reasons of personal safety, but mine was an automatic, not a revolver. I sure as hell wasn't in the habit of leaving it on my kitchen table in broad daylight for anyone to pick up and carry away. "Aren't you even a little curious, Lieutenant?"

Sam turned to look at me. "About what?"

"Who's trying to set me up for murder." I shifted in my seat, trying to ease the pressure on my wrists. "Who broke into my apartment to plant that gun there. Who wants me to take the fall for Felice Roarke's murder."

"Sure." He nodded. "Got any ideas?"

"I'd say Nicky Brooks except it's highly unlikely that he even knows where this place is."

Sam's expression gave nothing away. "That may be a possibility."

I knew what he was thinking. Nicky Brooks had no motive, and maybe I did. In my professional capacity I was involved, however peripherally, with the Roarkes. Vivian made no secret of her dislike for me, and it was a known fact that Felice had been emotionally unstable. The entire family disapproved of the insurance investigation and saw me as the one thing standing between them and a really big payout. Given these facts, someone could easily theorize that I'd killed Felice to get back at the Roarkes, but that was just it. Apart from their nearest neighbor, old Mr. Temple, and his granddaughter, Lois, nobody knew why I'd gone to the Roarke house in the first place.

It took scarcely twenty minutes for me to be photographed, fingerprinted, and searched. Then I was led down to a row of cells that must have dated to the Victorian era and shown into what was probably the drunk tank. I'd been in a similar place before, many years ago, when I was fourteen years old and my father was too inebriated on cheap wine to even stand upright.

It was Christmas Eve, and my mother had sent me down to the police station to get my old man out in time for midnight mass. It had been snowing lightly all day, the kind of gently drifting snow that lends an air of magic to even the most quotidian of streets, and the Bronx was lit up like Coney Island. I was alternately walking and running, slipping on the icy sidewalks, stopping under the streetlights to catch snowflakes on my tongue. At the corner of East 138th and Alexander, I jogged in place, waiting impatiently for the signal change. I ran up the front steps of the station, burst in through the double doors, and was halfway down the stairs when a big, burly Irish cop laid a hand on my shoulder and begged my pardon.

I'm looking for my old man. Dickie Boyle. Ma said he's in the drunk tank.

In the drunk tank, is he now? That's not a very respectful way to be talking about your father.

Just show me where he is, will you? I ain't got all night.

He took me down below to the cells and waited while I identified my father, sitting against a wall, his head resting on his knees. The warder opened the door, and I squirmed and elbowed my way through a mass of drunken, foul-smelling human flesh and caught hold of my father's arm.

Come on, for the love of God. Ma's waiting for you.

Leave me. Leave me alone. Let me stay here. He tried to pull away, but his alcohol-sodden muscles were no match for my adolescent strength. Besides, it wasn't the first time. I'd been to the police station at least once a week for as long as I could remember. I hauled on him until he stood up, then looped his arm around my neck and walked him out of the cell and onto the street, where he stood swaying, gaping openmouthed at the lights and decorations. *Is it Christmas already? It was Christmas just last week.*

"Never seen you here before." I turned and saw a wizened little man with a face so lined and seamed it was difficult to tell where his features began or ended. He was sitting on a three-legged wooden stool, wearing a motley arrangement of clothing. The top of his head was covered by a green knitted cap with an assortment of tiny brass bells fastened onto it, which jingled with even the slightest movement.

"Oh, hello. It's my first time, actually."

He grinned, then smacked his toothless gums together. "Haven't got neither drop of stuff, have ye?"

"Drop of…? Oh, you mean to drink. Sorry, I don't."

"So they picked you up just because." He seemed to find this funny. "That's not surprising. I think they does it so as to have something to do. Got to keep busy, you know."

"Yes, I suppose that's right."

Unlike the other inhabitants of the cage, he seemed to be clean and well presented, despite his outlandish attire. Even standing as close to him as I was, I could detect no foul odor, something that immediately recommended him to me.

"Don't know who I am, do ye?" He chuckled. "No, you're not from here. You wouldn't know that anyways."

I offered him a cigarette and lit it for him, then lit one for myself. "All right, I give up. Who are you?"

"My son, I'm the King of Newfoundland."

"The king, huh? I thought Newfoundland was under British rule."

"That's what they tells people." He drew on his cigarette and blew a long plume of smoke into the air. Over by the opposite wall, a fat man in a camel-hair coat stirred in his sleep and shouted out "Lorraine!" before lapsing back into silence. "They don't want no one to know."

"So I guess you, being the king, know lots of things that other people don't know." What the hell, I thought, at least he'd keep me entertained. "What do you know about the Roarke family?"

"The Roarkes?" He rocked back on his heels and crowed with laughter, slapping his skinny thighs. "The Roarkes? Oh, my son. If you only knew."

"Hey, I've got nothing right now but time."

He glanced around, obviously wary that someone besides ourselves might be listening. When it was clear nobody else in the cell cared one way or another, he beckoned me near. "Now mind what I tells ye. Because if they finds out I told ye this?" He made an exaggerated slashing motion across his throat with one finger.

I feigned shock and surprise. "That bad, huh?"

"Worse," he whispered. "Now then, the Roarkes. I suppose you knows that Mr. Roarke got everything he owns because he married her. She was the one with the money, not him. Her father must have owned half of Conception Bay, my son, but him? He had nothing. His crowd had already gone through whatever they had by the time he came along. Then he managed to get through what she had as well, this and that on the stock market, you know how that goes."

I remembered newspaper photographs of New York stockbrokers jumping out of windows after the crash of '29. "Yeah, I know how that goes."

"The oldest daughter—she's been married to God-knows-who, and more than once, I can tell you that. She always does the same thing. After she gets what she wants out of the fella, she gives 'im the heave-ho, you might say."

"That's terrible." I wanted to keep him talking. This stuff was better than gold.

"That whole crowd are in hock up to their eyes, my son. They're that desperate for money, they'd do anything."

"Anything?" If what he said was true, then Mrs. Roarke's unexpected death might service the double indemnity clause and relieve some of the Roarkes' financial woes. Killing someone for the insurance payout was so old it was practically a cliché.

"I puts nothing past 'em." He smacked his lips together. "Now, about that drink you mentioned."

"I'm sorry." I turned out my coat pockets to show him. "I haven't got a thing."

The man across the room laughed in his sleep, shouted "Lorraine!" again, and keys were being turned in the lock. Sam Lipinski motioned I should come out of the cell.

"Somebody pay my bail?" I asked as we made our way back upstairs.

Sam shook his head. "There's no bail. You were never arraigned and there's no charge."

I followed him over to his desk in one corner of a large room full of similar desks. The whole place was a cacophony of noise and apparent confusion and ringing phones. "Here," he said, handing me a sheaf of forms. "Sign these." He reached into his pocket and brought out a pen. "Stay away from the Roarkes."

"I can't do that, Sam." I signed my name with a flourish and gave him back his pen. "It's my job to investigate Mrs. Roarke's death. I can't in good conscience tell Columbia All-Risk to go ahead and honor the policy if I've got doubts about the validity of the claim."

He rubbed his eyes and stifled a yawn. "Frank, if I catch you hanging around and pestering these people, I'm going to have to bring you in."

I leaned close and grinned at him. "*If* you catch me."

He chuckled. "Got a ride home?"

"Not unless Crotty's has got a cab nearby."

He gave me a glance that spoke volumes. "Come on. I'll give you a ride."

I followed him out the front door and down the stairs to the parking lot. The city was silent and very dark under the blackout, the only illumination the thin sliver of automobile headlights allowed under wartime regulations. Sam unlocked the door, and I slid into the chilly car, my body reflexively retracting from the cold leather seats, my breath steaming out in front of me. He started the car, and we pulled slowly out of the lot, then turned left onto Harvey Road, its rows of chip shops and small mom-and-pop stores closed now, their windows dutifully covered with regulation blackout shutters.

Sam drove slowly, carefully, both his gloved hands gripping the wheel, but I could tell he was bone-weary, and it made me sad.

"Do you regret it, Sam?"

"Regret what?"

"Leaving New York to come to this place."

He turned onto Garrison Hill, and the big car's brakes groaned a little as Sam eased it down the steep incline. "This place ain't so bad."

"Seems like years ago, doesn't it? Instead of just months." Garrison Hill merged into Cathedral Street. We were moving steadily downhill, and in the distance, I could see the gleam of the moon reflected in the dark waters of the harbor. "Sam, what the hell happened?"

He glanced at me. "To what?"

"To us. Back there in New York, it seemed like we were—"

"Frankie, don't ask me that." His face twisted, and for a second, I could have sworn he was on the verge of tears. I was doing it again, pushing too hard, pushing too far, and going too fast. "For the love of God. I left because I had to. Not because I wanted to."

"Sorry." I reached across the small distance that separated us and squeezed his forearm. "Me and my big mouth, huh?"

"Aw, it ain't nothing." He steered us onto the long backbone of Duckworth Street, as dark and empty as the rest of the city. "Things happen. People change."

"Have you?"

He shrugged. "Maybe."

"Sam, I still—"

"What number on Water Street are you, again? It's up near the end, huh?"

I swallowed what I'd been going to say. "Yeah, couple blocks east of the train station." We slid gently down the long sweep of McBride's Hill and turned right onto Water. The bulk of a huge tramp steamer was silhouetted briefly in the gap between two

91

buildings, and I thought I could make out the figures of men moving about the deck. "Right here, just past the café."

Sam pulled the car up to the curb. "Safe and sound." He gazed out the windshield, not looking at me, his right hand fiddling with the bunch of keys hanging from the steering column. "Sorry we had to bring you in, Frankie, but you know the way it is."

I pushed open the door. "Wanna come up?"

He smiled sadly. "What for?"

I raised my hands in surrender. "Cup of coffee? Something to eat?"

"I shouldn't." He turned and gazed at me for what felt like an eternity. "But I will."

He left the car at the curb and followed me up the narrow stairs to my apartment. I yanked down the blackout blinds and turned on the side lamp next to the couch and the small kitchen light, but that was all. I took his coat and hat, hung them up, and ushered him into the living room. "It ain't much, but it's home."

He sat down on the edge of the couch, as if considering immediate and certain flight. His clasped hands rested on one knee as he glanced around the place. "It's nice. It's really you."

I found some coffee in the cupboard and filled the percolator, set it on the stove, and got busy fetching two cups. "You still take it black?"

"Aw, Frankie, these days I take it any way I can get it." He sounded bitter. Worse than that, he sounded lonely, and it cut me to the heart. "I probably got no right to tell you any of this, but I been mostly by myself since I came here… just gut-sick with being alone." He absently buffed his pinkie ring on the leg of his trousers. "I even started going to Temple again a couple weeks after I got here. That'd make my old man happy."

"I miss it too." I took out half a pie from the icebox and started slicing it up. "I guess you never really know what home is 'til you're not there anymore." I got sugar and cream for myself and poured hot coffee for both of us, brought the whole works of it out into the living room, and laid it on the coffee table. "I'm probably going to regret drinking coffee at this hour, but what the hell. It's not the only damn thing keeping me up tonight." I passed him a spoon and our hands touched. A sliver of pure, electric sensation coursed through me, and I was suddenly sitting next to him on the couch, pulling him into my arms, the coffee forgotten. His lips were hot, his body deliciously solid and real, and it was like I'd never left. The tip of his tongue insinuated itself into my mouth, and I opened wider, wanting him to take as much of me as he could get.

"No." He pushed me away and got up quickly. "Forget it, Frank. I should go." He wiped his mouth on the back of his hand. "This isn't gonna work."

"Sam."

"I said no." He looked around for his coat. "What are we doing, huh? Trying to turn back time?"

"It's got nothing to do with time, Sam." I went to where he was. "This is you and me. This is *us*. Goddammit, you saved my life in New York—"

"I almost got you killed in New York, you dumb schmuck."

"Sam, I don't know anybody in this town. You know what that's like. For Christ's sake, I don't expect us to go back to the way we were—"

"Shut up." He took hold of my lapels and pulled me into him. "You never know when to shut up."

"What I'm trying to say is—" But I couldn't say anything, because Sam had me in his arms, making me remember why I was so crazy about him in the first place. I clutched him like the lifeline he was, crushing him against me while he did amazing things with that gorgeous mouth of his. The next thing I knew I was flat on my back and Sam was on top of me and we were more than a little disheveled.

"Frankie...." Sam shifted his weight, sending a frisson of gorgeous sensation through me. "Frankie, maybe we shouldn't—"

I pulled his head down and kissed him, groaning as I felt the hot, slippery intrusion of his tongue. I tangled my hands in his thick, black hair and held our heads together, prolonging the caress until he was breathless. "Goddammit, Sam, I want you. Christ, I've always wanted you. What the hell are we waiting for?"

He stood up, his eyes dark with desire, and held out his hand. I went into his embrace and we kissed again, bodies swaying together as to some internal rhythm. His cock was hard, making a nice bulge in the front of his trousers, and he smelled like aftershave lotion and good tobacco. I slipped his shirt buttons free and leaned in to kiss the point of his bare shoulder. "Frankie…." He moaned softly as my fingers flicked across his nipple. "Take me to bed."

He didn't have to tell me twice. "Yessir, Lieutenant." I grinned. "Right away."

In the privacy and darkness of my bedroom, he stripped me like we'd been lovers all our lives and he'd done it a thousand times before. He pulled my shirt off my shoulders, running his fingers lightly over the scars on my torso. "Aw, Frankie…."

"Don't," I whispered. "That was the past. It's over now. This is us, Sam. This is me and you."

He was lean and muscular, with a dancer's taut planes and angles and an enviable flexibility. He touched me in places I'd never been touched before and did things nobody else had ever done, licking and tonguing and caressing until I was a shuddering heap, begging him for what I'd wanted as long as I could remember.

"You sure about this, Frankie?" He hovered over me as I lay on my belly, his lips lightly touching the back of my neck.

I could feel the tantalizing pulse of his hard cock against my skin, and it wasn't enough. I wanted him in me. I wanted to feel him. "I'm sure." The ragged, hungry tone of my own voice surprised me. "Please, Sam. Do it."

There was a pause and his warmth withdrew. "Frankie, you ah… you got anything?"

"Drawer. I think there's some Vaseline…." My desire was a living thing, a hungry animal. I wanted him so badly speech was an intolerable burden. The drawer opened and closed, and he was back, and there were warm fingers gently opening me, stretching me, smoothing the rough edges.

"Relax, baby." His lips ghosted against the nape of my neck. "It's me. It's Sam."

I forced myself to breathe. He slid a little further in and suddenly it didn't hurt anymore. He made a small throaty sound and my cock twitched. A warm wave was rising up from my thighs, mounting into my belly, and I thrust back against him. The familiar contours of my bedroom shattered into lines and shadows as we moved together, our skins slippery with sweat, oblivious to anything else but this. Sam was hitting something deep inside me and it was filling me up with a pleasure that was keen and violent. He thrust into me, arching his back, and I heard him cry out, a ragged sound that had my name in it, and then I was there too, tipping over the edge into a hot, wet space that ravished me to silence.

I lay in the dark for a long time while my body slowly groped its way back to sanity, my skin full of tiny twitches and tics. I turned my head and Sam was there. "Sam."

His face was close to mine, his gaze suddenly intense. "Guess we did it this time, huh?"

My gut clenched. "Are you sorry?"

He grinned. "Nope." He leaned in to kiss me, and it was okay—no, it was more than okay. It was pretty damned amazing. "You know, it's been ages since I did that." His grin turned into a laugh. "I guess I ought to do it more often."

I leaned in and kissed him. "Yeah. You should." A feeling I'd been holding on to for years warmed me deep inside. *I love you.* I didn't say it out loud.

"Aw, Frankie…." He opened his arms and I went into his embrace. "Listen to me." He caressed my arm gently with the backs of his fingers. "You promise me something?"

"Anything." I grinned. "Within reason."

"I want you to promise me that you'll be very careful."

"Why?" I couldn't resist. "Afraid you got me knocked up?"

"Frank, this is serious." He drew a slow breath. "Be careful. Watch where you're going and… don't step into any darkened doorways."

"You know something." My heartbeat sped up 'til it was thudding violently against my ribs. "Who is it? Who's after me?"

He cupped my chin in his hand and kissed me gently. "There's been some talk that Nicky Brooks caught wind of our idea and hopped an airplane to Gander."

The warm, easy feeling evaporated. "So if that sick son of a bitch decides to throw slugs at me some sunny afternoon, what then?" I got up and yanked on my bathrobe. "Maybe I should put on my Sunday best, sit around and wait for him?"

"Oh, come on!" Sam sat up and threw back the bedclothes. "Jesus, Frank. I'm behind the eight ball here. It's not like I can warn him off. If Brooks does decide to look you up, he's putting himself directly in my line of fire. The Constabulary'll have him behind bars in a heartbeat." He reached for his clothes and started getting dressed. "Maybe he'll come after you, but there's no way in hell he's gonna get to you." He didn't bother unbuttoning his shirt but just pulled it on over his head. "I can give you protection, if that's what you want."

"Yeah, some wet-behind-the-ears constable who'll light out for parts unknown when Nicky shows up with his goons." I reached for my pack and lit a cigarette. "And you're okay with this?"

"Frank." He came toward me, but I turned my back on him.

"You'd better go now, Sam. I think you can find the door."

"All right, Frankie, if that's the way you want it." His voice was flat, uninflected. "I think I probably can."

Chapter Seven

IT FELT good to be back in old New York, back among the familiar streets where I'd grown up, playing stickball in the vacant lots and stealing apples from old man Schultz's store. I turned a corner and stepped into Lipinski's butcher shop, thinking I'd pick up a nice roast to take home to Ma. She'd been working real hard lately, and I wanted her to have something nice, a good meal for a change.

I heard the little bell tinkle on top of the door as I went in, and Dutch Lipinski smiled at me from behind the counter. Dutch was wearing his usual apron, but this one had "Be Happy" printed on it in bold black letters. "You," he said, pointing at me. "Come here. You I've been looking for. Listen to me." A door opened somewhere in the back of the shop, and a young man stepped through. "You know my son, Sam?" Sam was about twenty-two, with thick, curling black hair and a tightly groomed mustache, and lashes long enough to qualify as sinful. "You and Sam, you work it out. I got nothing to say about it."

Then the shop went away, and I was lying in a rumpled bed in a small apartment high above the city. Sam Lipinski was lying beside me, his tongue curling around and around my nipple while one hand worked my cock in a slow, luxurious rhythm. I started to say something, but he kissed me, and the kiss went on and on, and his hand sped up, and I came with a groan that woke me up just in time to hear the phone ring.

It was still dark outside, not even the tiniest slit of light showing underneath my blackout blinds. I rolled over and picked up the phone. "Yeah?"

"Did I wake you up?"

"Sam? What time is it?" The luminous numbers on my alarm clock told me it was 5:00 a.m.

"They pulled a body out of the water down in Quidi Vidi." He sounded tired, and I wondered what time they'd called him out of bed. "It matches Mrs. Roarke's description."

I pulled on my clothes and fumbled around in the dark 'til I got the gas lit in the kitchen and made myself a quick cup of coffee. There was no time for a shave, but I did it anyway, somehow managing not to cut my own throat in the process. In less than half an hour, I was out the door and flagging down the single cab that just happened to be cruising down Water Street. "Take me to Quidi Vidi?"

"Sure thing, mac." The driver's gaze met mine in the rearview mirror. "Hey, Frank! How's tricks?"

I knew that voice, and in spite of circumstances and the ungodly hour, I laughed out loud. "Goddammit, Mark Donnelly. What the hell are you doing here, boy?"

He grinned. "Last time I saw you, you were working for Nicky Brooks."

"Christ, it's good to see you." I meant it. Don't get me wrong, St. John's is an all right town, but it couldn't hold a candle to the old, familiar streets of New York. "What brings you all the way up here? You don't look like an enlisted man."

"Oh, I was in for a while—marines. Did some time in Guadalcanal and got sent home on an honorable discharge." He claimed he'd come here chasing the wartime boom and ended driving a hack for Crotty's. "Kind of a screwy town, but I like it. Reminds me of the nastier parts of Brooklyn, you might say."

In less than five minutes, he had deposited me in the part of town known as Quidi Vidi, an ancient fishing village around which the city had reportedly grown up. It had been settled by itinerant English fishermen back in the days when settlement in Newfoundland was discouraged—sometimes at the point of a rifle— and even now it retained much of its eighteenth-century character, especially in the cheery little houses and the narrow streets.

Now, however, there was nothing charming about it. A phalanx of constables stood around a tarpaulin-wrapped bundle on the ground. To one side, Sam Lipinski was speaking quietly to Sergeant Picco. The latter saw me and turned away with an expression that told me I was not welcome.

"I thought you might appreciate being involved," Sam said, after we'd shaken hands. Seeing him like this was surreal, when mere hours ago, we'd been making love in my bed and murmuring endearments. "The owner of the pub—" Sam pointed up the road to where a low, squat white building huddled against the side of a hill. "—had just closed up and was walking back home when she noticed something floating in the water."

"Uh-huh." I looked past Sam to where a heavyset middle-aged woman in a rumpled raincoat was speaking to two constables, a cigarette dangling from the corner of her mouth. "She just noticed it. Sure."

He gave me a look. "This isn't New York, Frank."

I ignored the look and his tone. "So she just noticed something in the water, and she called the constabulary." I nodded toward the bundle. "Mind if I take a look?"

He shrugged. "Suit yourself. Hey, Ryan." A slender young constable detached himself from a group and came over. "Let Mr. Boyle take a look, will you? He might be able to help us identify the body."

The body. It's funny how that phrase so readily marks out the dead from the living. While we're alive, we're people. We've got habits and personalities, likes and dislikes. As soon as the lights go out, we're nothing but an empty sack of flesh. I crouched beside the body and waited while a constable peeled back the tarpaulin. The first sight of a corpse—and I've seen plenty—always sends a shudder through me. You think you're prepared, but trust me, you aren't.

She hadn't been in the water long, judging by the appearance of the body. There was the usual white foam in her nostrils and mouth, probably tinged pink by her lungs bleeding, although in this light, I couldn't tell. By that token, she'd been alive when she went in the water. I reached in and raised each eyelid in its turn, ignoring the hissed curses around me, but the light was too poor for me to make anything out. "Murder?" Sam had been hovering over me the whole time, and I addressed this remark to him.

"No. No, there's no evidence for that and even less likelihood, given the circumstances."

"What do you mean?"

"Frank, the homicide rate here is less than one murder a year. Even with the wartime influx of Americans and Limeys, it just doesn't happen here the way it does back home." Sam flipped his notebook shut. "Suicide, most likely. Death by misadventure. Maybe she had one too many at a dance and slipped into the Gut"—this was the local name for Quidi Vidi harbor—"on her way home."

"Yeah." I stood up, my knees and back protesting about how I needed to find myself a gym somewhere and get back into shape. "She's young—was young." And pretty, not that it would do her any good now.

"So—not the woman of your dreams?" Sam stifled a yawn with the back of his hand.

"No." I shook my head. "She's not Mrs. Roarke."

Sam nodded at the constables. "All right, boys, wrap her up again."

"Look, Sam." I didn't quite know how to frame it, only that I didn't like the way we'd left things. "You wanna get some breakfast?"

"Sorry, Frank." It was curt and noncommittal. "I got work." It was also, I realized, a dismissal. He turned to Picco and said something about the woman's body, and just like that, it was like I didn't exist.

By now a few feeble streaks of dawn were beginning to lighten the sky, and I could see well enough to find my way back to the road. A solitary Crotty's cab was idling, the driver sitting with his cheek pressed against the window, sound asleep.

I rapped on it, waking Mark Donnelly. "Don't you know you can die that way?"

He blinked at me. "It's okay. I got it in neutral."

I couldn't help myself. I laughed. "Take me to the Heartache Café," I said, sliding in on the other side. "Breakfast is on me. I'll stand you to a real feed."

We drove through the morning streets in relative silence, save for the muted murmuring of the cab's radio. Mark was sleepy-eyed and yawning, and I suspected he'd been on duty all night, but he accepted my offer of breakfast with amiable good cheer. We took a booth near the windows where we could sit and watch the traffic crawl up and down Water Street. There wasn't much happening at this hour, and Jack had only just fired up the kitchen, so we had to wait a bit for breakfast. But there was plenty of hot coffee while we waited, and it was good to listen to Mark reminiscing about New York. It wasn't long before we'd exhausted all our talk about sports, drinking, the weather, and the war, and pretty soon the conversation turned to personal matters.

"So what's the deal between you and this Lieutenant Lipinski?" Mark asked, shoveling a huge forkful of egg into his mouth.

I made my face as blank as possible. "I don't follow you." I took a sip from my cup. "Damn, this coffee is real good, isn't it?"

"You know what they'll do to you if they catch you around here." He reached for a piece of toast and spread it thickly with strawberry jam. "All's I'm saying is—don't." His gaze held mine, and I wondered what he wasn't telling me.

I decided to take the risk. "Something you want to say, Marcus? Maybe you better spit it out." My heart was hammering in my throat. I knew what he was going to say, and I didn't want to hear it, because hearing it would mean he'd figured it out, and if someone like him—a man I knew only as a casual acquaintance—could get beneath my surface like that, anybody could.

He leaned over the table and spoke confidentially. "Maybe back home in New York you had some kind of deal with the cops—split the profits, that sort of thing, and that's fine for the Bronx, but, brother, you try that sort of setup here, and they will have you in the clink so fast your head'll spin. From what I've seen, Lipinski's as straight as they come. You probably know why he left the 40th Precinct."

I knew no more than Sam himself had told me. "He got out of line, that's what I heard. The precinct made things a little hot for him."

"He decided to be the one-man clean-up crew. Nearly got himself permanently cleaned up, if you know what I mean."

Sam had told me he'd spent time in the hospital, that he'd been threatened, but that was about as much as I knew. He'd made it sound like the same kind of stuff that had always gone on in the neighborhood. "I know some guys beat him up."

Donnelly's expression was sardonic. "Yeah, that's one word for it. The way I heard it, they nearly killed him. They didn't think he was gonna pull through. Soon as he gets home, someone lobs a cocktail through his bedroom window and burns the place to the ground. Word on the street is he's a dead man from the inside out. See, it ain't your usual hood on the street that wants Lipinski dead—it's the cops."

"The police? Why on earth would they want to kill him?"

Mark looked up as Chris DuBois appeared to refill our coffee cups, smiling his thanks at the handsome bartender. "Because

Lipinski got in too deep and went where he wasn't supposed to go. He got busy turning over rocks, you might say. You might also say he turned over the wrong ones and found something he shouldn't have."

"Graft?" It wasn't unheard of. You might think otherwise, but police officers—at least the ones I knew—always had their hands out.

"Ohhhhhh yeah." Mark laughed. "New York—at least the 40th Precinct—got too hot to hold him. When the job opened up here, he took it. If he hadn't, he'd be dead by now."

"Dead?"

He nodded. "Oh yeah. Dead. They were gunning for him but good." He glanced at his watch. "Frank, breakfast was excellent, but I gotta go. There's a nice soft bed somewhere with my name on it." He moved to take out his wallet, but I stayed him.

"Skip it. This one's on me, remember."

He grinned. He was a really good-looking guy, and the smile did incredible things to his smooth, mobile face. "Thanks."

"Just answer me one thing."

He got up and took his coat from the hook. "Sure."

"How come you know all this stuff?"

Again with the grin. "Good friend of mine's a private dick. Sam Lipinski hired him to give the 40th the dust. My friend's the kind of bird that don't miss much. He takes a slant, and whatta ya know, there's more than a few of 'em bent. They made it real tough on him, so tough he finally hadta leave." He shrugged. "So now you know. I'd be careful around Lipinski. If you're not on the square, he'll nail you for it." He laughed good-naturedly. "Maybe he'll nail you anyways." He gave me a little mock salute and was gone.

I sat for a while, taking my time with the coffee, watching as Water Street filled up with people and traffic and the sun rose higher over the city. I wondered what Sam was doing, where he was now, if he'd gone off shift or if he was still standing by the water in Quidi

Vidi, trying to find out all he could about the drowned mystery woman. Did he regret last night? Was he wondering about the things we'd said and how we'd left it? Come to that, where did we stand now? I was pretty pissed off with him, knowing as he did that someone meant to do me harm but not bothering to tell me who it was. It was okay for him to cite police regulations and the exigencies of an ongoing investigation, but I was the one with a target on my back. Come to that, so was he. From what Mark Donnelly had told me, it was even money which one of us got it first.

I bought a copy of the *Evening Telegram* from a newsy standing in front of the Bowring Brothers department store, and wouldn't you know it, right there, smack on the front page for all the world to see, was a picture of me and the headline, *POLICE SUSPECT AMERICAN IN ROARKE DEATH.*

Great.

I WAS walking down Water Street one cold, bright day in mid-December, and I'd stopped to wait for the traffic to part long enough to let me through. The wind was out of the northeast and cold enough to break your bones. I'd left my office wrapped up to the ears, wearing my warmest coat and with a wool muffler wound around my neck, but it didn't come close to dispersing the chill. New York was cold in the winter, sure, but this was something else again. Maybe it was the city's proximity to the North Atlantic or maybe the way the wind got trapped and funneled between the hills; either way, I was shivering inside my clothes by the time I got to the spot where Baird's Cove meets Water Street, and seriously reconsidering my decision to walk back to my office.

I was standing hunched inside my overcoat when a hand curled around my elbow and a body insinuated itself into the space beside me. "Hey, Frankie."

For a split second, I thought it might be Sam—we were standing directly opposite the courthouse, and it was reasonable to think he'd have midday business there—but the voice wasn't Sam's voice, and the man standing beside me, pressing the nose of an automatic into my ribs, wasn't Sam Lipinski.

It was my old pal Nicky Brooks.

"Fancy meeting you here." It went without saying that he'd found me—then again, Nick always was the smart one.

He smiled. "I missed you, Frankie-Boy. What can I say?" The gun jabbed me, harder than was necessary. "What say we take a little walk, me and you?"

"You're barking up the wrong tree, Nick. They don't go for that sort of thing around here. You'd better put that thing away before somebody gets hurt." I kept my eyes on the traffic cop, willing him to turn around and see me, willing him to wonder what the hell I was doing, standing frozen on the sidewalk in the middle of the day—but then I remembered this wasn't New York, and a loitering pedestrian in St. John's, Newfoundland, doesn't mean a whole hell of a lot to local cops. Like as not, he figured I was passing the time of day with a friend, so I wasn't getting any help from him.

"Just shut your trap and walk, Frank. It's loaded and I will blow a hole in you. I ain't never lied to you before." Again the predatory smile, the animalistic flash of white teeth. I didn't have to wonder what I ever saw in him; I knew.

We walked east along Water Street, passing various shops and businesses, heading toward the gun emplacement on the Hill O' Chips. The sentry saw us pass, but he merely nodded and touched his cap before resuming his perusal of the North Atlantic. I was being abducted in broad daylight in what should have been the safest city in the world and nobody was doing a damned thing about it.

At the easternmost extremity of Water Street, near the harbor, a car was waiting. Nick pushed me into the back seat ahead of him, and then he got in, the gun still trained at my ribs. A second man was at the wheel, patiently smoking a long, thin cigarette. He wore a navy pea jacket and one of those wool caps the merchant seamen wear, pulled down low over his eyes. I couldn't see too much of his features, but I noticed a thin mustache and a scar running diagonally from the corner of his left eye across his face, ending just above his top lip. His skin was badly pockmarked, or maybe they were acne scars, and one eyelid drooped more than the other did. I took a mental photograph, remembering something Charlie had told me: *Don't bother writing nothing down. Develop your memory instead. You remember something, nobody can't take it away from you.* The driver nodded at Nick in the rearview mirror, and for a second, I could have sworn there was something familiar in the gesture. "Where to, Nicky?"

"Point it up the hill and get us out of town. Just drive. I'll tell you when."

The driver yanked the stick, and we lurched forward to the sound of gears grinding. Nick swore and thumped the back of the driver's seat with his free hand. "Come on! You think this is some kinda joke?"

The car shuddered into motion and up the hill, traveling in an easterly direction, which meant we were probably going to Logy Bay or Outer Cove, or any one of the numberless small fishing villages scattered around the outskirts of the city. Staying within the city limits meant he wanted to question me, maybe work me over a bit, but Nick was going out of town, probably to knock me off. I thought wistfully of Sam and hoped he wouldn't be the one to find my body.

We drove for perhaps three-quarters of an hour through thickly forested wilderness punctuated with the occasional small house or barn. Ahead of us in the distance, I could see the ocean, so we were traveling north, away from the city. This meant nothing much except that they'd probably dispose of my body in the ocean when they were done with me.

"Bring your swimming trunks, Nicky?" I turned my head to look at him, but he was staring out the opposite window at the passing view. "Kind of cold for a dip this time of the year, or maybe you wanna die of exposure?"

"You talk too much." He jabbed the gun barrel into my side. "Maybe you want a couple new slugs to match the ones the docs took outta ya?"

"That'd be just your style, Nick. Shoot first."

Nick kicked the back of the driver's seat. "This is the place."

The driver hesitated. "Are you sure? There's supposed to be a red house right before the turn, and it ain't there."

"Do what I tell you," Nick snapped, "and quit yappin' about it. This ain't no radio show!" The car turned onto a narrow, dirt road, shuddering over several large ruts. We had changed direction again, heading away from the sea.

"You shouldn't have come here, Nicky." I smiled at him just like these were old times and this was a friendly conversation we were having. "I never figured you for a moron, but I guess I was wrong. Don't you know they got cops up here too? Good ones. They're gonna bury you."

"Only one getting buried here today is you, Frankie. Or did you think I'd forget it was your testimony that sent me up, huh?"

"You killed my little brother."

"From what I remember, you were there as well, Frankie." The gun barrel moved to stroke my cheek, and I shuddered in spite of myself. Was I attracted to him because he was dangerous, because he possessed the kind of virile, explosive sensuality that captivated me and drew me in? Maybe what I felt for him wasn't attraction at all but nostalgia, some remnant of the love that had existed before his hired thugs had gunned down a member of my family.

Leo had just turned seven the year he died—the year he was gunned down in cold blood in front of Phinster's drugstore in the Bronx. I'd been seeing quite a bit of Nick, both in and out of bed, and had firmly established myself as one of his best errand boys. When he asked me to help him out on a little job one night, I'd readily agreed. I'd done jobs for Nick before: running money uptown to the bank or collecting what he was owed from bettors. For months now I'd been a doorman at his club, allowing entry to Nicky's friends and business associates and bouncing out anybody who didn't behave themselves.

Sure, Nicky. Anything you say.

I want you to teach some wise guys a lesson, Frank. Can you be here tonight, around eight?

I went home and kept my mouth shut, just like Nicky told me to. I'd been getting a wash at the bathroom sink when my sister asked me where I thought I was going. *It's a school night, Frank. You said you'd help Leo with his homework.*

I got things to do. Don't be pestering me.

I know the kind of business you got. You make me sick, you know that?

Leo had come into the bathroom to watch me get ready. He was just a little guy, kind of small for his age but bright. We all figured Leo might be going places. *Where ya going, Frankie? When are ya coming back?* He'd showed me a slingshot he had: *I won it from Jimmy Turpin, fair and square, playing bottle caps.*

I remember I got mad at him, told him he shouldn't be gambling, yelled at him. *Get outta here! You wanna end up like the rest of these no-good bums around here, huh?*

I went over to the bookmakers and waited around, just like Nick had told me to. A bunch of the usual guys were there, cracking jokes and smoking, and one of them said to me, *You coming with us, Frankie, or are you gonna stand around all night staring at your shoelaces?* There was a car waiting by the curb, and I got in. Some of the guys had violin cases and some others had burlap sacks lying on the floor by their feet. I wasn't stupid. I knew the way things worked, and I understood what was going to happen here.

We'd driven through my neighborhood, passing stores and tenements and old Mrs. Temmolini's fruit stand on the corner. Just as we got to Phinster's drugstore one of the guys said, *Slow down, Joey, there he is.* A big man wearing a pinstriped chesterfield and smoking a cigarette had been standing in front of the store. Some small boys were playing nearby, shooting marbles on the sidewalk. The guys all reached down and took their tommy guns out of the violin cases and the burlap sacks.

Just then the car slowed enough so I could see the group of boys as clear as day. One of them was my brother Leo. He'd seen me in the car, and he started forward. *Frankie, hey Frankie, where you going, Frankie?*

The bullets had been meant for the big man, but the first rounds caught Leo in the chest and stomach, stitching him across, nearly cutting him in half. He was probably dead before he hit the ground. I didn't wait for the car to stop. All I could think was I had to get to him before it was too late. If I got to him in time, I could help him, I could make the bleeding stop, make his heart start beating again. I tore open the door and ran to where he was, but there was nothing I could do. There was nothing anybody could do. He was already gone.

Nicky had showed up in the hospital while I sat outside in the corridor, my clothing stained with Leo's blood. I still don't know why I was waiting. What was I waiting for? The doctor had taken one look at Leo when I brought him in and shook his head. *That kid's dead. Sorry.* I hadn't waited for an ambulance but had flagged a taxi and come straight to the hospital with Leo in my arms. His little body was cold, and he was already getting stiff, but I told myself it was nothing. Some medicine, maybe some oxygen out of one of those fancy tanks and he'd be just fine, he'd be better than fine.

The doctor's pronouncement struck me like a slap in the face and I started yelling at him. *Whatta ya mean? He's gonna be okay. Give him some medicine.*

Something in the way I said it or the way I looked as I said it must have resonated with him. He stopped and stared at me like I was out of my mind. *Look, kid, I'm sorry. There's nothing anybody can do for him. Is there someone I can call for you?* It was absolutely final, and I remember wondering who the hell this guy thought he was, saying such a thing. Leo wasn't dead. Leo was alive. Leo was playing marbles down on the corner in front of Phinster's drugstore with the other kids. Leo was shooting bottle caps in the alley behind our building and waiting for me to get off work so he could climb up into my lap and read the funny papers with me. Leo wasn't dead. Maybe that's what I kept telling myself as I sat there in the hospital corridor, or maybe I was waiting for somebody to explain it to me.

Nicky came and sat beside me, clean and beautifully dressed, a gorgeous apparition. *I'm sorry, kid. Jake didn't see him. You know how it is.*

I have to tell them. I couldn't get the picture of Leo crumpling to the ground in a hail of bullets out of my mind. It would haunt my dreams and wake me screaming for the rest of my life. *I have to tell them.*

Tell who, kid?

I gotta tell my family Leo is dead.

Two weeks later, Nicky's case came up for trial. I stuck around long enough to get myself subpoenaed to testify. Once Nicky Brooks was sentenced and safely on the train to Sing Sing, I packed a few things in a rucksack and climbed out my bedroom window. I had just enough money for a ticket to California, and for the next twenty years, that's where I stayed—learning my trade at the hands of one of the best private dicks in the business and biding my time. I figured when Nicky Brooks got out of Sing Sing, I'd be ready for him.

See how well that turned out.

The car pulled up in front of a battered-looking old barn leaning precipitously to one side, located in a clump of beech trees bare of most of their leaves. Nicky nudged me out at the point of his gun, and I went, stumbling over the unfamiliar terrain. The inside of the building was as dark as the black hole of Calcutta, and I moved forward carefully, uncertain of what I might find underfoot. There weren't, as far as I could tell, any animals in the place, but there had been something living there recently, if the smell was anything to go by. I didn't know much about livestock, but I knew manure when I smelled it.

The driver had shut off the engine and come in behind us, shadowing Nicky and me but not saying anything. He and Nick took hold of my arms and flung me down onto a chair. Just in case I had any ideas about escape, they lashed me tightly to its wooden frame, my hands cinched behind me. I heard a match being struck and then a small gas lantern flared into life, illuminating the interior of the barn. It was the kind of place I'd gotten real familiar with during my time in California: a ramshackle old building that's been abandoned and left empty, located on some nearly impassable back road far enough away from civilization so nobody can hear you scream. Outfit the inside with a few strategically placed beams, some metal rings set into the walls, or whatever suits your fancy, and you've got yourself a purpose-built torture tank.

"So, you just gonna keep me here?" I asked.

"Don't worry. I'll make sure it's a real comfortable stay," Nick replied. He was busy filling a syringe with what I guessed was some kind of drug to either knock me out or make me talk.

I'd been with him once, back in New York, when one of his bully boys had ventured too far to one side of the invisible line separating Nick's business from the rest of the underworld. Nick had dispatched a couple of torpedoes to pick him up and bring him to Nick's private office in back of The Dive. Like most of Nick's surroundings, it was sumptuously furnished, beautifully decorated, and soundproof. You could take a guy in there and chop off each of his fingers with a cigar cutter and nobody would ever hear him scream. I know. I saw Nick do it once. Nick had injected the man little by little while the guys worked him over. When the man started to pass out, Nick would shoot him full of amphetamine to wake him up, just so he could feel the pain.

"What's it gonna be, Frankie?" Nick nodded to the driver, who leaned down to roll up my sleeve. "You want I should give you a little of this and just let you spin for a while, before me and Tony here give you the works?"

Tony… so the driver's name was Tony. I told myself to remember this because it might be real important later on. The driver got behind me and was fiddling with my cufflinks, rolling up my shirtsleeves. He was clumsy. He dropped something into the dirt by my feet and had to bend and pick it up. As he came up, he swayed toward me, and I caught the barest breath of sound: "Hold on, Frankie. Gonna be okay."

Easy for you to say, I thought. I felt the pinprick of the needle in the bend of my elbow as Tony injected me, and I braced myself, but nothing much happened.

Nick's hand slid into his coat pocket and came out wearing brass knuckles. "So tell me, Frankie." Nick's tone was light, conversational. Yeah, we were just two good buddies having a pleasant chat. In a filthy barn. In the back of the beyond. While I was tied to a chair and injected with dope. "Who's in charge of the supply around these parts?"

That threw me for a loop. "Supply?"

His metal-covered fist smashed into my face, knocking my head back, and suddenly there were little stars around me.

I shook it off and spat out some blood. "You'll have to do better than that."

He grinned. "You always were a hard nut to crack. Who's in charge of supply around here? Huh?"

"No idea." When his fist slammed into me this time, it felt like my skull had cracked wide open. Something shattered way in the back of my mouth, and I felt grit on my tongue. There was more blood this time, most of it from my nose, which seemed to have burst wide open like a popped balloon. "This how you're getting your kicks nowadays? I guess the Spinelli brothers gave it to you good."

That drew him up short. "Spinelli brothers?" He glanced at Tony. "What the hell are you talking about?"

The pain in my face momentarily faded to a dull roar. "The Spinelli brothers. They took over your territory while you were inside. That's why you had to leave New York."

"Leave New York?" He laughed unpleasantly. "Somebody gave you a wrong steer, Frankie-Boy." Nick paused long enough to shrug out of his jacket and loosen his tie. He had that manic gleam in his eyes I knew so well. He was enjoying this. "Is it coming in on the train? Who's in charge of it? Do you know?"

"Nick, why don't we just cut to the chase before you wear yourself out?"

He slammed me again, then brought up his foot and kicked me hard in the chest, knocking me over backward. Tony came running to pick me up again, and I wondered why the drug he'd given me wasn't working. What had I been injected with? If Nick was trying to get information out of me, he could do better than this. "Who's in charge? Do the cops have a hand in it?" He swung at me, catching me high up on the temple. "Goddammit, Frank! Somebody got into my supply lines, and now I can't move no product in or out of here. You and that kike cop—what did you do? You son of a bitch, this is costing me plenty!"

It occurred to me that maybe he meant the black market. I flashed back to that conversation I'd overheard in the Heartache Café, the day Felice Roarke was killed. Jack had said that St. John's was as much in thrall to black marketeers as anywhere else nowadays: *I guess we got much the same thing here that goes on anywhere else: silk stockings, chocolate, booze, you name it. The cops try to crack down on it, but they can't be everywhere. A lot of these gangster types from the States caught wind of what was going on here and followed the band....*

"You should have stayed in your own backyard, Nicky." That last hit was acting on me like an opiate, and I wondered how much longer I could stay conscious. My face throbbed in time to the beat of my heart and that kick in the chest hadn't done me much good, either, but suddenly I was laughing.

"What's so goddamn funny?" he snapped. "You gone screwy or something?"

"Sam Lipinski," I said. "Sam Lipinski is gonna kick your ass."

He drew his arm back to clobber me and several things happened simultaneously.

The barn door blew open, disgorging a whole lot of cops. Nicky shouted, "It's that goddamn Yid. Somebody tipped him off!" And Sam was there, grinning at Tony the driver, who was rubbing at his face with a handkerchief, wiping away makeup and false facial hair.

"Sorry about the subterfuge there, Frankie, but it hadta be done." Mark Donnelly grinned down at me, sticking his soiled handkerchief in his coat pocket. "I hope Nick didn't bust you up too bad."

It made me laugh in that weak, semihysterical way people have when their brains have shut down and some other, much more primitive part of them has taken over. Sam untied me and I tried to stand up, but my legs collapsed, and I fell flat on my ass. I watched Alphonsus Picco putting the cuffs on Nicky as Nicky screamed and yelled that he was going to kill "every single one of you Newfie sons of bitches," and then Sam and Mark were helping me into an ambulance that waited just outside in the lane.

I CAME to myself what felt like hours later but was probably days, and realized there was a clean cotton sheet under me rather than sawdust and filthy straw. I was at home in my apartment, lying in my own bed with the smell of antiseptic in the room. Somewhere a radio played quietly, and underneath, I could hear the sound of dishes clinking in a dishpan full of water. Someone was singing along with the song on the radio, a jazzy version of Cole Porter's

"Let's Do It." I lay very still and listened. It was Sam. He was washing my dishes and singing in my kitchen. He had a hell of a voice, and I remembered how he'd always be practicing when we were kids, how he wanted to be on Broadway and make it to the big time. Did he regret choosing police work instead of following his dream? He would have been a sensation on Broadway.

"You should be resting." The bedroom door opened and he was there, shirtsleeves rolled up over his elbows and his collar open. "How are you feeling?"

"Like somebody stomped on my face." I wondered why he was lingering in the door like that. "How long have I been out?"

"Would you believe three days?" Sam grinned. "You were sleeping the sleep of the just, Frankie. Mind if I come in?"

"Sure." I was naked under the bed covers, and I was pretty sure he'd stripped me. "How did you know where I was?"

"Mark Donnelly has been acting as our go-between. He's a pretty smart kid, that one. Started out driving a hack in Brooklyn. I never saw anything like him. The kid's absolutely fearless." Still he hung back, fiddling with the objects on my dresser. He looked everywhere but at me. "We wanted to give Brooks enough rope to hang himself." He wandered over to the window and stood there gazing out. "Guy by the name of Tedesco was a button man for Brooks, right up until Brooks decided he was bent and went to work on him with brass knuckles and a broken wine bottle. Nearly killed him too. While Tedesco is recovering in hospital, he receives a surprise visit from an old school pal of his, Joey Spinelli. Tedesco's had just about as much of Brooks as he can stomach, so he spills. Spinelli's trying for as much of Nicky Brooks's property as he can get. He finds out I'm here, so he gives me the heads-up. Donnelly is just a nice little bonus who got tired of driving in New York and decided to try something different."

"He saved my life." I figured this time I owed him more than breakfast. "Hey, Sam, why don't you come over here where I can see you?"

He hesitated. "Maybe that's not such a good idea. The way we left it last time...." He shrugged. "You could say I'm the reason you got your head kicked in."

"If you hadn't put Donnelly on my trail, I'd be dead by now." I held out my hand. "Come over here." Still he hung back. "Please?"

He came and sat on the edge of my bed. "Frank, I wanted to tell you everything, I really did, but I couldn't jeopardize the investigation." He pleated the edges of the sheet, his head bent. "You know, I seen a lot of things in my years on the force, but seeing what Brooks did to you, it just took the heart out of me. I'm serious."

I patted the mattress beside me. "Why don't you get in?"

"I think you need your rest."

"Come on, I won't break." He leaned forward, and we melted into each other. He was warm and he smelled good, and the press of his body against mine was absolute bliss. I pulled him tight against me and wrapped my arms around him. Holding Sam was like coming home after being exiled in some hostile foreign land for a long time.

He drew back and looked at me. He was pleasantly flushed. "I don't think this is such a good idea, Frankie." He made to get up, but I held on to him.

"Why not?" My whole body was throbbing. I wanted him so much. "You suddenly change your mind about us?"

"You're not well. That goon nearly beat you to death. Dammit, you should have been in the hospital."

I smoothed his cheek with the backs of my knuckles. "Come off it, Sam. I'm a big boy. I can take care of myself."

He gazed at me for a moment, and when he spoke, his voice was husky with desire. "That's what I'm afraid of."

As far as athletic lovemaking went, this wasn't it. There were no clashing cymbals, no pounding drums, no rockets' red glare, but I didn't give a damn. Lying there with him naked next to me was more heaven than any guy deserves. We spent a long time just touching each other, and being together in that quiet space lovers know as bliss. I caressed his chest and shoulders, the hollow of his throat, and his flat belly. The skin of his cock was exquisitely sensitive, and when I touched him there, he moaned, long, shuddering sounds that pulsed in the bottom of my belly and tingled in the tips of my fingers.

I took him into my hand and worked him slowly, stroking him until he was close to the peak of his desire, then letting him down again. His slender body writhed and heaved beneath me and he cried out as he came, his fingertips pressing hard into my shoulders. When I moved up to lie beside him, he wrapped me in his arms and held on tight.

"You know there ain't never been anybody for me," he said. "Not like this. Not like you and me, Frank." He reached between my legs to touch me, and I held his wrist, guiding his hand. His mouth was against my chest, his tongue caressing my nipple, and my release crashed over me: devastating, brilliant. I lay for a long time with my head against his shoulder, vaguely conscious of his fingers in my hair, his mouth pressing kisses against my forehead, my cheek. "You feel okay?"

"Mmm…." I traced the indentation of his breastbone. "Better than okay. You're really good at this, you know?"

He laughed. "So you've been telling me. You better be careful, or you're gonna make my head swell up, you know that?"

"Sam, I—"

He laid two fingers against my lips. "Don't." His expression was suddenly grave, and all his former good humor had vanished. Seeing him so serious frightened me.

"Sam, what is it? I was just gonna say—"

"I know what you were gonna say." His dark eyes were sad. "Please, Frank, just don't."

It went through me like a spear, but I kept it to myself. "I'm glad you're here, Sam."

His smile was sad. "Yeah."

We were quiet there, alone together in the dim light, and there was more I wanted to say but I didn't. I knew I didn't have the right.

Chapter Eight

TO CELEBRATE—or maybe because he saw what was in my icebox and felt sorry for me—Sam treated me to a romantic dinner at the Heartache Café. It was a chilly Saturday night, and those few local inhabitants who'd braved the cold were sensibly warming themselves in any of the cozy pubs on George Street. My face still looked like I'd gone ten rounds with Jimmy Braddock, but I didn't care. Knowing Nicky the way I did, I knew he'd come after me again as soon as he was out, but I'd be ready for him. I was with Sam, I loved him, and that was good enough for me.

"You happy?" Sam reached under the table and squeezed my knee. We knew Jack was sympathetic, but neither of us was under any illusions. Men who felt like we did about each other ran a very real risk of being beaten to death and dumped in the harbor.

"Delirious," I grinned, and we both laughed.

"You are a sarcastic son of a bitch, you know that?" Two other couples occupied tables close to the rear of café, and a man in his early fifties sat by the window reading the newspaper. Sam looked up as Chris appeared at our table, bearing a nice bottle of wine. "Hello, Chris. How's tricks?"

The handsome bartender grinned. "I'm hitting on all eight." He tilted the bottle so Sam could read the label. "Is this what you wanted?"

119

Sam nodded. "That's perfect. I don't know how Jack does it, what with rationing and all." He raised an eyebrow. "He's not up to anything illegal, is he?"

Jack came out from the kitchen, a towel slung over his shoulder. "And if I am?"

Sam pretended to be hunting for his badge. "Well, I'd have to run you in, Mr. Stoyles. You see, we are under wartime rationing in this town."

"Uh-huh." Jack gave him a wink. "Is that what they're calling it these days?" He nodded toward me, his expression grave. "You guys better turn down the shine. You might as well be wearing signs saying you're on active duty."

I froze. "Really?"

Chris exchanged a look with his boss. "Yeah." He shifted uncomfortably. "There's not many people in here tonight, but you better put a pin in it. You know how it goes." He reached out and squeezed my shoulder. "You guys take care, huh? Enjoy your meal. I know Jack's got something special."

Sam leaned toward me. "Jack would know, trust me." He reached for the bottle Chris had left and poured for both of us. "Dishonorably discharged on a blue ticket." Sam's voice was very quiet. "You know what that means?"

I searched my memory. "Yeah, I think I heard something about that. They booted him out because he—"

"Yeah, because he—you got it." He nodded toward my glass. "Good wine?"

"The best." I turned the bottle and read the label. "Jesus, Sam, can you afford this on a cop's salary?"

He pretended to be offended. "You saying I can't afford you?"

I had a witty rejoinder all ready, but the sight of a tall man in a dark overcoat hovering near our table stopped me cold. "Yes?"

"Are you Frank Boyle?"

"Yeah."

"Frank Boyle, the insurance investigator?" And, when I'd asserted that this was indeed the case, he said, "You've been served, Mr. Boyle."

"What the hell…?" I took the envelope, tore open the flap, and drew out a single sheet of paper. "In the magistrates court at St. John's, Newfoundland…." I showed it to Sam. "What the hell is it?"

He scanned it briefly. "Restraining order, or possibly a cease and desist. I'm not up on English common law." His expression was sardonic as he passed the paper back to me. "Who'd you piss off this time?"

I read the rest of it. "The Roarkes, by the look of things. No big surprise there. Listen to this: 'You are hereby ordered to cease and desist any contact with the Roarke family, resident at 27 Kings Bridge Road, St. John's, Newfoundland.' Can you believe this? They're ordering me to stop investigating them." I tossed the paper down onto the table. "Still think they've got nothing to hide?" Koestler was going to shit a hairy canary.

Sam gazed at me, one eyebrow lifted. "I never said they had nothing to hide. You know what I think?"

"Tell me."

Sam took a mouthful of wine. "I'm not divulging any big secret when I tell you that whole family is strange—not just odd, but suspicious."

My scalp prickled, the way it always did when something big was happening. "Yeah?"

"I went back through the files to see if there was anything there. I didn't find too much, except…." His dark eyes twinkled. The bastard was holding out on me.

"Dammit, Sam, if you know something—"

"The youngest daughter, the late Felice Roarke, liked to take her clothes off in public. She was arrested last July in Bannerman Park for putting on a show for several servicemen. This past October, at a formal dinner at the mayor's house, she stripped naked and dove into the swimming pool."

"The swimming pool? In October? It's a wonder she didn't come down with pneumonia."

"The mother was practically a recluse, only rarely going out into society." He swirled his wine in the glass, watching the patterns it made. "The oldest daughter—she's a bit more difficult to figure."

"Vivian?" I remembered her long fingernails gouging my face. "She might be the only sane one in the family, and that's saying something."

Jack arrived and along with him came dinner, and what a repast it was: crown rib roast with tiny potatoes and fresh local carrots, everything cooked to perfection. I stuffed myself to the point of embarrassment and sat back, wondering whether it would be less than polite to unfasten the top button on my pants.

We polished off the last of the wine and grinned at each other. "Dessert?" Sam asked.

"No, sir." I held up a hand in protest. "No, thank you. One more bite and I'm liable to start stripping off my clothes."

"Not even a sweet? Frank, you disappoint me." He grinned. "But it helped you forget about that nasty old cease and desist, didn't it?"

"What cease and desist? The next thing you know—" The next thing I knew, the front door opened and Eamonn Molloy of all people stepped in. He shook the chill from himself and rubbed his hands together, making a show of blowing on them to warm them. Jack had seated us toward the back of the Heartache, and I hoped Molloy wouldn't see us.

I hoped wrong. "Frankie, me boy!" He came toward us, all smiles. "How are you getting on? And Lieutenant Lipinski! Now what are the odds of us three meeting up here?" Chris was polishing glasses behind the bar. Molloy raised his arm and snapped his fingers imperiously. "How about another chair over here, if you aren't too busy." He snickered. "Lazy cunt," he murmured. Chris brought a third chair, and Molloy sat down, unbuttoning his coat and draping it over the back of a vacant seat nearby. "It's nice to see my boys getting along, so it is. Lipinski, you're not scheduled to work tonight, are you?" His smile was dazzling and wholly predatory, the grin of a shark right before he bites your head off.

"No, sir." Sam exchanged a glance with me. "I worked last weekend."

"Ah, right, so you did, so you did." Molloy leaned toward me, blocking most of Sam's view with his body. "You're looking well, Frankie. I was sorry to hear what that punk Nicky Brooks did to you." He reached out and caught the point of my chin between his thumb and finger. His eyes as he gazed at me were shallow and much too bright, and I wondered if he had been drinking. I couldn't smell it on him, but then again, not everybody sweats their whiskey like my old man did. There were times when my father, recovering from his latest bender, would lie on the sofa in the front room, stinking so strongly of booze it all but colored the air around him.

"Thanks for your concern." I tried not to sound sarcastic when I said it. Eamonn and I hadn't formally parted ways, but his increasingly bizarre behavior had lessened his appeal considerably. "Excuse me. I'm going to the bathroom."

The men's room in the Heartache Café was located at the back of the building and shared a wall with the kitchen. As I stood there washing my hands at the sink, I could hear Jack and Chris talking as clearly as if they were on the other end of a telephone. What they were saying made my ears stand up but good.

"I still don't think you should trust him." The deeper voice—and the Louisiana drawl—belonged to Chris. "He's a peeper, and you know what those guys are like. One wrong word to him, and this whole thing blows sky-high. What do you think Sam'll say, huh? Never mind the guys back in Cairo."

"He's an insurance dick," Jack said. "Not the same thing, and anyway, I know this guy. He's on the level."

"You don't know," Chris replied. "You've seen him, what? A handful of times?"

"I *know*." Jack was emphatic. "I got a gut feeling." There was a pause, and I heard rustling noises, the sounds of cupboard doors opening and shutting. "I say we bring him in."

"I think maybe you ought to talk to Sam before you do anything rash," Chris said. "North Atlantic Command might not be too keen on you divulging family secrets. And you know what they say about military intelligence… dammit, Jack, there's a war on." There was a longer pause and his voice went away, so I hurried it up, dried my hands, and went back to the table.

Eamonn was sitting there by himself. Sam was nowhere to be seen. "I like it when a man intuitively knows he's not wanted," Eamonn said. "Now let's me and you get down to a little business, Frankie. Perhaps we could reconvene at my place?"

Something hot and red pulsed behind my eyes, and I felt my hands curling into fists. "Where is he?"

"The kike you were sitting with? I sent him on his way with a flea in his ear." He pushed Sam's empty chair with his foot, none too steadily. He was definitely drunk. "Sit down a wee while, Frankie."

The hot redness throbbed and thundered. God, I wanted to plant a fistful of knuckles right in his smirking face. "What did you say to him?"

"I told him the truth." He shrugged. "Being that I'm his superior officer, he was inclined to believe me. He's a good cop, but he's not the sort a man like you should be associating with." Eamonn sat back, one arm draped negligently over the back of Sam's empty chair. "Now, why don't you come and sit down?" I took my wallet out and started toward the bar. "He already paid your bill," Eamonn called.

I turned in midstep, snatched my coat and hat off the coat tree, and was out the door.

The street was dark and empty, about as quiet as it gets. A thread of melancholy music drifted down from somewhere—a radio in somebody's apartment, maybe, or one of the bars on George Street—and a lone taxicab crawled east, its driver slumped against the window with one hand on the wheel. My breath steamed out in front of me, and I shivered, buttoning my overcoat tightly. Where the hell was Sam? What had Eamonn said to him that made him bolt?

Sam's apartment was on Gower Street, on the top floor of an old Victorian, so it made sense that he'd have gone uphill, heading for home. I stuck my already-chilled hands in my pockets and started after him. Trying to find his particular footprints in the sea of pedestrian treads left on the snowy sidewalk was hopeless, so I trusted to my instinct. It occurred to me Eamonn might have taken a notion to follow me, and part of me hoped he would. Police chief or no police chief, I'd enjoy smearing him over a nearby wall.

I headed straight up Prescott Street, following the steep pitch of a hill that made me feel like I was back in San Francisco again. The cold wind tore at my face and knifed through my overcoat, chilling me to the bone. At the corner of Prescott and Gower, I turned right and kept walking 'til the big hotel on Cavendish Square was in my sights. Sam's house was opposite a steep little street called Nunnery Hill.

I rang the bell and waited, and when there was no answer, I pushed open the outer door and went up the dark, narrow stairs to his flat. "Sam?" I tapped lightly on the door, not wanting to disturb the other inhabitants of the house. "Sam, you in here?" I tried the knob. It turned and the door swung open. Sam's apartment was quiet, and a single bulb burned in a small lamp set on a table against the wall. A pack of Sam's cigarettes lay on the kitchen table and the glass ashtray had three butts in it. The bottom of it was faintly warm to the touch. I went down the hallway to the bedroom, but the bed was made, the covers pulled tight.

I don't know what made me turn just then—maybe there was a small sound, or some noise from the street outside flicked a metaphorical fingertip against my subconscious—but I did and headed back up the hall toward the bathroom. There was a strange smell in the air, like iron mixed with washing soap and a soupçon of aftershave powder. I pushed open the bathroom door, and the first thing I saw was a foot, elegantly shod in a brown wingtip shoe, and a man's prone body. My gaze traveled until I got to his face and saw the thin line of blood snaking down his temple, and I knew the worst had happened. Sam Lipinski had been shot.

"No! Jesus, Sam." I went down on my knees, but I knew not to touch him. He was breathing, a shallow rattle that didn't reassure me one bit. I caught hold of his wrist, feeling for a pulse. His skin was warm, reassuringly alive, but his heartbeat was faint and thready. "Sam, don't move. If you can hear me, don't move, okay? Just… stay there."

SOMEHOW I found the phone, rang Grace Hospital, and told the operator to send an ambulance, a cop had been shot. Then I went into the bathroom and lifted his head into my lap and held on, wondering what I should do, wondering if there was anything I could do, or if the time for doing things had come and gone already. I laid two fingers against his neck and felt a subtle, reassuring throb underneath the skin. He was alive… against all odds, he was alive. The blood from a second wound stained the pale-blue cloth of his shirt just below his left shoulder. Clearly his assailant had been aiming for the heart.

"Sam." I lifted each of his eyelids, but who was I kidding? I didn't know what I was looking for. How did you tell if somebody was asleep, unconscious, or dead, and anyway, his heart was beating. The side of his head was matted with dried blood, but he was alive, he was breathing, so maybe there was hope that he would be all right, that he would get up and move around under his own power, that perhaps he wouldn't end up a drooling cripple in a care home.

"Hey." The sound of his voice, weak but nevertheless Sam, startled me. "Frankie."

"Don't try to talk." Jesus, there was so much blood, just too much blood. "Stay still. The ambulance is on its way."

"Wasn't real sure." He caught hold of my arm. "I knew it. I knew it. No way it could—" He coughed: a wet, racking noise. "No way."

"Sam, baby, please don't talk."

"Shot me."

There was a scuffle on the stairs, and I called out that he was here, come up here, and suddenly the place was full of guys in white coats, and firemen, and cops.

Alphonsus Picco was at my side, his notebook already open. He stood with me and watched as they loaded Sam onto a stretcher. "Did you do this, Boyle?"

"What?" I turned on him, outraged, my hands still wet with Sam's blood. "How the hell can you even ask such a thing?"

He gazed at me with cool eyes. "It's my job." He nodded to the stairs, down which they'd just taken Sam. "He'd ask the same thing and you know it."

"Yeah, I just…." My legs were too weak to hold me. I staggered over to the couch and sat down. "I came in here and found him." I ran the whole thing through for him, how we'd had supper at the Heartache Café, how Eamonn had showed up, and when I came out of the men's room, Sam was gone.

Picco's pencil paused over his notebook, hung in midair for a moment. "Captain Molloy was there? At the café?"

Something in his tone alerted me. "Why is that strange?"

"Captain Molloy was on duty 'til six this morning. I find it odd that he'd leave his post."

So did I, but I wasn't interested in discussing it. "Listen, Picco, how about I take some of Sam's things to the hospital? I'm sure he'll be needing them."

The young sergeant shook his head. "Nope. This entire apartment is the scene of a crime. I can't allow anything to be taken out of the building. By rights I should detain you but…." He shrugged, as if he knew detaining me wasn't going to do any good.

"You're a friend of Lieutenant Lipinski. Go on to the hospital if you like, but leave everything here as it is."

He didn't have to tell me twice. "Thanks, Sergeant."

"Get out before I change my mind."

I found a cab circling the block and hailed it. No Mark Donnelly this time, just some old local guy, half asleep and cranky at being drawn out of his reverie. When he let me off in front of Grace Hospital, I tossed him an extra two bits just for luck. I wasn't in any mood to tempt fate. I needed all the good fortune I could muster.

The girl at the information desk was singularly unhelpful, but she did confirm Sam had been brought in and was being assessed prior to surgery. I asked if I could see him, but she gave me a look that could peel paint. "Sure, go on in," she snarled, "pull up a chair in the operating room. Tell 'em Shirley sent ya." She snapped her gum. "Go over there and sit down out of it. I'll ring the charge nurse on the surgery floor and tell her you're asking after him."

I was covered in Sam's blood and in a mood to push back. "Can't I go up there and wait for him? I promise I won't cause any trouble."

"No, you can't." She looked me up and down. "What in the name of Jesus happened to you, anyway? You get into it with a couple of longshoremen?"

"It's a long story."

Something in my face or my voice must have given it away, because she said, "You're the one who found him, aren't you?"

I nodded, not trusting myself to speak.

"Is he your friend?"

"Yeah." I took out my handkerchief and scrubbed at the drying blood on my hands. "Yeah, he's my friend."

She glanced around, then summoned me over. "Go in there—" She gestured toward the public washroom, located down a narrow hallway just past the desk. "—and get cleaned up. I'll let you wait for him, and when I get the all clear, I'll let you go upstairs. Maybe I'll tell them you're his brother or something. What about that?"

"Thanks." Her kindness nearly reduced me to tears, and I turned away before she could see the effect she'd had on me.

It was a long night. I sat for hours in the waiting room, watching people come and go, stretchers being wheeled in and some being wheeled out again. Nurses went by on silent feet, moving swiftly from one place to another at the urging of the PA system, and now and then, a harried-looking doctor appeared, stethoscope slung around his neck. I waited in a numb stupor while Sam's blood dried on my clothes, running every scenario I could think of through my mind: Sam was dead; Sam was a cripple; Sam would end up a drooling idiot, locked in a care home 'til the end of his days. Thoughts chased themselves around and around in my head until I felt like Nicky and his boys had laid into me again. It was a hell of a way to pass the hours.

I must have dozed a little, because the next thing I knew, the girl was shaking me awake and the clock above the reception desk read six thirty. The sky outside the windows was still dark. At this latitude it wouldn't get light for at least another hour and a half. "You can go up and see him now, if you want to."

I rode the elevator up to the sixth floor and identified myself to the charge nurse, a stern-looking woman of perhaps fifty years of age with a thick Scottish brogue. "Are ye related to him?"

I hesitated for an eye blink. "Yeah, I'm his brother."

She looked me up and down. "Ye look nothing like him."

I shrugged. "He's adopted." I decided she was going to let me in or I was going to raise holy hell out here in the corridor.

"Mm. Well, go in, but no longer than ten minutes, and I'll be watching the clock." She pointed down the corridor. "Third door on your right."

"Thank you."

"*Quietly*, or else." She turned back to her paperwork.

You know those movies where the hero pushes open the hospital room door and his beloved is awake, smiling, and happy to see him? This wasn't like that. The side of Sam's head was swathed in bandages, his skin dyed with that stuff they use for disinfectant. A deep-purple bruise the size of my hand extended across his face like a remembered slap, and his closed eyelids were swollen. His breathing was even, but with an underlying rattle that gave me the willies. His bare torso was wrapped in bandages, and a drainage tube came out under his left arm.

"Oh, Sam." Seeing him like this was a real punch in the gut. I just wanted to go find whoever was responsible for this and give them the works. I sat down in the chair next to his bed and watched him breathe for a while, reassuring myself that he was alive, that he'd survived, and he was going to be okay—something his attacker hadn't counted on. Whoever had burned the powder on him probably figured Sam was dead and all his troubles were over, because a dead cop wasn't liable to put the finger on anybody.

"Frankie…?"

It was barely a breath of sound, but I heard him. I took hold of his hand and squeezed. "I'm here, Sam." The press of sudden tears burned the backs of my eyes. "I'm right here, baby."

He raised swollen eyelids and gazed at me. "Shot me."

It was the same thing he'd said back at the apartment. "Don't try to talk."

He drew a wheezing breath. "Men… clothes. Tell Picco. Thirty-eight."

"Okay, Sam." I held his hand against my cheek. "I'll tell the chief."

"Not Molloy." He squeezed my fingers. "Picco." Then, drowsy from the anesthetic, he faded back into unconsciousness before he could say anything else.

EAMONN MOLLOY was still in his office when I walked in without knocking. He was sitting at his desk, surrounded by stacks of paper and opened file folders, a pair of reading glasses perched at precisely the right angle on his nose. He looked up, apparently without surprise. "Ah, Frankie, me boy. Finally came to your senses, did you?" He gestured at an empty chair. "Have a seat. I've just got some paperwork to get clued up here, and then maybe we can go and have a drink."

"I'm not interested in drinking with you."

"Are you not? That's a shame." He pulled his glasses off and tossed them on the desk. "I was thinking a wee dram of whiskey might be just the thing, followed by—" He gave me a knowing smirk. "—a little bit of the old slap and tickle."

I was around the desk and had the front of his shirt clenched in my fist before he could blink. "Was it you?" His head made a satisfying noise when I shoved him back against the wall. "Did you do it?"

He caught hold of my hands, but I wasn't letting go. "What, Frankie?" He offered me his most conciliatory smile. "Did I do what?"

I gazed into his eyes and saw nothing there except his usual predatory self-interest. "Sam Lipinski is in Grace Hospital." All the fight drained out of me and I let go of him. "Someone shot him."

"Is that right?" He smirked. "Dead, is he?"

I weighed the consequences of assault on a police officer very carefully. Yeah, I weighed them for about half a second before I hauled off and belted him in the mouth. "You slimy son of a bitch! That's what this is all about, isn't it?"

There was a sudden flurry of running steps and Picco was there, framed in the doorway. "Boyle! For the love of Christ, what do you think you're doing?" He was reaching for his handcuffs when Eamonn called him off.

"It's all right, Sergeant." Eamonn patted my back. "Mr. Boyle and myself were just having a friendly disagreement." He slung an arm around my shoulders. "Isn't that right, Mr. Boyle?"

"There's blood on your mouth," Picco said grimly.

Eamonn's grip tightened until the hard muscles of his forearm were pressing against my windpipe. "Not at all, Sergeant. Not at all. Merely a little disquisition between friends."

Picco glanced at me, made as if to say something, and then forgot about it. "Captain Molloy, are you sure—"

"Of course, my boy. How's that drowning case coming along? Any leads?"

"No…." Picco knew something wasn't right, but he wasn't about to disobey a direct order. "Nothing yet, sir."

"Well, keep me informed." Eamonn released me and held the door for Picco, then closed and locked it behind him. "You've a temper, Frankie. You need to be watching that." He grinned at me, and there was something wild and unreasonable in his eyes. "Did you get your little missive from the Roarke family?"

"That was you?"

He shrugged. "Not directly. It takes a judge to issue a restraining order, and as you can see, I'm but a lowly policeman, dedicated to the public good."

This was a laugh. The only good Eamonn was dedicated to was his own. "It's my job to investigate the Roarkes. For all I know, Mrs. Roarke is holed up in the basement, subsisting on last year's rhubarb jam."

"Did the Jew boy tell you all about the Roarkes?"

I winced. "They're all nuts."

Eamonn shook his head. "You mustn't cast aspersions, Frankie. It's a bad habit you have, judging people the way you do. All you Yanks are like that, aren't you?" He raised an eyebrow. "Poor Vivian, now, she was married to a Yank, and that accounts for much in the way of family troubles. She's never quite forgiven him."

"Just what are you getting at?"

He touched his bleeding mouth, rubbed the blood between his fingertips, and looked at it. "Do you know, Frankie, if you'd done that to me in Kilgarvan, I'd have fucking *killed* you." He surged toward me, pushing his fingers into my face, smearing his blood on my mouth like some bizarre tribal ritual. With both hands he grabbed the back of my neck, pulling me toward him. He held me to him and kissed me savagely, so hard it hurt. "You shouldn't go saying things, Frankie." He squeezed my face, digging the tips of his fingers into my cheeks. "You should use that sweet, sweet mouth as it's meant."

I stumbled back, away from him, tripping and nearly falling over the chair. "Oh boy, have you got the wrong number." I was itching to give him a little more chin music, but we'd already been there, and hitting him again wouldn't solve anything. "For a nickel I'd paste you again, except I haven't got the time." I straightened my tie and shrugged my jacket back up where it belonged. "If Sam Lipinski dies…."

He laughed. "You'll what?"

I unlocked the door and tore it open. "Go to hell."

"That's the spirit, Frankie!" He called after me, loud enough for the entire building to hear. "Find yourself another kike!"

Eamonn's office was set well back from the rest, at the rear of the building and overlooking Military Road. To reach the exits, I had to pass through the main reception area, the place where everybody went to register complaints, and the same area I'd passed through the night Sam and Picco had arrested me. At barely eight in the morning, it was mostly deserted except for an old man in a heavy overcoat, a working girl with the remnants of a fight smeared across her face, and Vivian Roarke.

She saw me and turned away, but she wasn't fast enough. I caught her by the arm and spun her around. "Lovely morning, Miss Roarke. Or is it Mrs. Brooks?"

"Mr. Boyle, do you mind? You're hurting my arm."

"I don't mind at all. How come you're here?"

She wrenched away from me and spoke to the sergeant at the desk. "Captain Molloy, please." She looked impeccable, not a hair out of place—although it was unusual to see a woman wearing slacks in public.

"Molloy, huh?" This was something new. "Since when are you so tight with the police?"

She didn't blink. "I'm sorry to hear Lieutenant Lipinski was shot. I hope he's doing better now."

Something cold was crawling up between my shoulder blades. "How the hell did you know about that?"

She gazed at me coolly. "A girlfriend of mine lives in the building. She heard the shot. We... were talking on the telephone when it happened."

"Uh-huh."

"You don't believe me."

My fists clenched. "Say, how's your crazy mother doing up there in the attic, huh?"

Twin spots of hot color bloomed high up on her cheekbones. "You disgust me."

"Go bury your sister." I was on my way through the swinging doors, almost out of range, when she fired her parting salvo.

"I feel sorry for you, Mr. Boyle. You can't see what's right under your nose."

#

THE funeral for Felice Roarke was held three days after the first of the brand-new year at St. Thomas's Anglican Church, just up the street from the Roarke house and close enough to the houses of other eminent families that they couldn't miss what was probably the social event of the season. I parked my rented car in front of the hotel and walked north toward the church. I figured if I kept out of sight, I might get a chance to observe the proceedings without attracting undue attention. If the Roarkes had been angry enough to have me served, it was probably better to stay out of their immediate sight.

Both sides of Kings Bridge Road and as far south as Duckworth were crowded with cars, and the church parking lot was full. Anyone who was a friend of the Roarkes—or pretending to be—was here today in their best bib and tucker. I slipped into the building and took a seat near the back, pretending to busy myself with a hymnal from the rack in front of me while I took a good look around. The Roarke family—minus Mrs. Roarke, of course—sat at the front, heads bowed. Vivian Roarke was wearing a long-sleeved black dress and a black hat with the sort of brim that dipped low on her forehead, shielding her features. She was accompanied by three other women, probably Roarke cousins. Mr. Roarke sat on the other side of Vivian in a somber navy-blue suit. His head wobbled on his neck, and I wondered if he was weeping or if he'd maybe drunk too much. Everybody deals with grief differently. Obviously the Roarkes were able to parcel theirs out: Felice warranted a lavish final affair while the supposedly dead Mrs. Roarke had been handed off like somebody's dirty laundry, without so much as even a notice in the *Evening Telegram*. And they wondered why they were under suspicion?

Doctor Elmer Nichol had wedged himself in against Mr. Roarke's side, although the pew was hardly large enough to accommodate Vivian, the three Roarke cousins, Mr. Roarke, and the young doctor. He was sobbing loudly into a voluminous handkerchief, his features wrung by a grief a little too dramatic to be real. I remembered the erotic painting of Felice he had hung in his office, all nubile promise and silken skin in a mummer's costume. Would he cry himself to sleep tonight, weeping over all his dirty pictures? Old Mr. Temple was nowhere to be seen, nor was his granddaughter, Lois.

The smell of the church was like the smell of churches everywhere: old paper, dust, and furniture oil overlaid with a patina of beeswax. I told myself it was okay, I could take it, but as soon as the organ began to play, I started to shake. I clasped my hands together in front of me and forced myself to breathe: in and out, in and out. This wasn't Leo's funeral. This was somebody else. They weren't going to bring in Leo's casket today, and that wasn't my sister up there at the front of the church, sobbing her eyes out. It wasn't my brother who'd been gunned down by Nicky Brooks's mob, not this time. Not Nicky Brooks.

Nicky Brooks. What the hell…?

He'd come in by the same door I had and was walking up the center aisle, hat in hand, dressed in an impeccable dark topcoat with a dark suit underneath and a black tie. Nothing but the very best in mourning attire for Nicky Brooks. After all, he had a lot of practice at this sort of thing. I wondered what he was doing out of jail. I figured Eamonn Molloy and his boys would have sent Nicky back to the Bronx. The fact that he was still here pointed to strange doings. By rights, he should have been back in New York by now, under glass.

What had Alphonsus Picco said, the night Sam was shot? Eamonn Molloy was on duty all evening. So how come he'd shown up in the Heartache Café while Sam and I were there, and how did he know we'd be there in the first place? Of course he was the chief of police, with more latitude to wander, but still. What else did Eamonn know about Sam and me? Was my apartment being watched? Was Sam's? If Molloy was bent—and I had good reason to suspect he was—then Sam and I were in a lot of trouble, maybe the kind of trouble we didn't want, the kind we couldn't handle.

Nicky slid into a pew about halfway up the church, nodding to an elderly couple who'd moved over to make room for him. He took his topcoat off and slung it over the pew in front of him and sat down before I could check for the telltale bulge of a gun under his arm. If I knew Nicky—and I knew Nicky, probably better than anybody—it was there. He didn't go anywhere without a piece. He even slept with one underneath his pillow at night. I just hoped he wouldn't take a notion to shoot the place up.

There was a rustle at the door and I turned. The casket had arrived and was being slowly wheeled up the central aisle by two mortician's assistants, both dressed in mourning black, both wearing pure-white gloves. The casket was white, surmounted with an enormous spray of flowers. I stood with the rest of the congregation and watched it pass. There was Felice Roarke, or what was left of her. If there was any mercy in the world, maybe she was finally at peace.

The priest, following close behind, was a tall, thin man, quite elderly, wearing gold pince-nez and carrying a prayer book held out before him like an offering. He reached the altar, turned to the congregation, and indicated by a gesture that we should sit down. "I am the resurrection and the life, saith the Lord. He that believeth in me, though he were dead, yet shall he live, and whosoever liveth and believeth in me, shall never die."

My throat closed together, and I bit hard on the inside of my cheek. I don't cry easily, and I hadn't cried in years, not since Leo died, but I almost lost control of myself then. I thought about Sam, lying in the hospital, and I thought about my mother being lowered down into the cold ground. I could see the dirty street again where Leo's body lay, open eyed and broken, his blood puddling around him in a crimson pool, and I remembered thinking maybe if I scooped it up, put it back inside him, and then he would be fine, he would be all right. But his body was limp and nerveless, and whatever elusive thing had animated him was gone. He was gone. He was dead like Felice Roarke was dead... Felice Roarke, slumped back against the seat of her expensive English roadster, a bullet in her forehead and a silk stocking knotted around her slender throat.

"I know that my redeemer liveth, and that he shall stand at the latter day upon the earth. And though this body be destroyed, yet shall I see God: whom I shall see for myself, and mine eyes shall behold, and not as a stranger."

A silk stocking tied around her throat....

I remembered something Jack Stoyles said to me one day in the Heartache. We were talking about the black market and whether it affected people here the way it did elsewhere. *A lot of these gangster types from the States caught wind of what was going on here and followed the band*, Jack had said. Gangster types. He'd been careful to stipulate that gangsters—American gangsters—had a hand in the illegal trade around here. Then there was the conversation between Jack and Chris, the one I'd overheard the night Eamonn had chased Sam away: *He's a peeper, and you know what those guys are like. One wrong word to him and this whole thing blows sky-high.* What was he talking about—and what had Jack meant when he'd said he wanted to bring me in? The deeper I got into things around here, the more complicated it got.

I was having a hard time keeping track of all the players. Felice Roarke, dead in her car with a silk stocking tied around her throat. What did it mean? A joke? A message? Whoever had killed her hadn't bothered with the niceties but had put a bullet into her brain at point-blank range. Her killer had shot her—literally— between the eyes. In order to get that kind of accuracy, he'd have to be either one hell of a good shot, or sitting so close he couldn't miss… sitting, it turned out, in the front seat of Felice's own car. It was true that most people are killed by someone they know and there is rarely anything random about a "random killing." I'd be willing to lay odds the police already had a prime suspect in mind and were just waiting for the right time to bring him in.

Nicky Brooks turned around in his seat and, seeing me, gave a little smile and a wave. Behaving this way in the middle of a funeral was wildly inappropriate, but he knew that. Nicky might have come from the gutter, but he'd adapted well to being on the fringes of polite society. There were even a few members of the upper crust who'd let him into their houses now. I watched him and I didn't signal back. My body still hurt from the beating he'd given me in that empty barn, and I wondered how long it might have gone on if Marcus Donnelly hadn't rescued me. Nick probably wouldn't have beaten me to death, but it would have been close enough. Nick was good with his fists and didn't have any problem using them; it was rumored he'd once considered a career in the ring before vice and all its delicious accoutrements beckoned.

The funeral ceremony was too long, but they always are. When it was over, I was sweating and my collar was distinctly uncomfortable. I watched Felice's coffin pass by, the solemn procession of the funeral cortege filing silently out of the church before I turned to go.

"Hey, Frankie." The words were a mere puff of sound, less than a whisper in my ear, but I stiffened. "Let's talk." His fingers closed around my elbow, and I didn't have to turn around to know there was a gun in his other hand. I knew this because it was sticking in my ribs. He pushed me ahead of him, out the front door and around the corner past the parking lot. "Now we can have a few words like gentlemen, without fear of being interrupted."

"Don't be an idiot, Nick." I jerked my chin toward Kings Bridge Road. "The place is swarming with people. Do anything to me and the cops'll nab you in a minute."

"You afraid of me, Frankie?" He reached around with his other hand and caressed my side. "You didn't use to be. You used to beg me for it. At least that's how I remember it."

"Did you kill her?"

He laughed, an unpleasant sound. "Now, why would you ask me a question like that, Frank?"

I grunted as the gun was shoved harder into my side. "Seems to me you're as likely as the next guy. The cops probably think that too. Did you wait 'til the signal turned red before you popped her?" He'd have had to be sitting in the front seat right next to her, with the gun in his hand, ready and waiting. Maybe he even said something to her, something that made her turn to face him with her hands still on the wheel.

"You wanna keep still, Frankie. I'd hate to blow a hole in you."

"Get your paws off me." I stepped to one side, twisted away, and caught his gun hand at the wrist. I'm sure we made quite a picture, two grown men grappling with each other in broad daylight in a church parking lot on the fourth of January, when the rest of the city was still celebrating the Christmas holiday. I held him in the painful joint lock Charlie had shown me all those years ago, releasing him only when I had secured his weapon. "Now get lost."

He straightened his clothes, smiling the sinister, thin-lipped smile I knew so well. "Whatever you say, Frankie, but you know me. I'll be back." He leaned in, his face so close to mine I could see his pores. "And next time I won't be this gentle." He gave me that strange little wave and turned on his heel. I watched him go until he rounded the corner of the church and vanished from my sight.

"Mr. Boyle."

Vivian Roarke? Her sudden overture startled me, to say the least. "Miss Roarke. My condolences for your loss."

She was as beautifully turned out as ever, but her gaze was shadowed by a sorrow I knew all too well. "Thank you for coming. It's most decent of you." She extended her gloved hand, and I shook it. The gesture had the flavor of a tacit apology, but with Vivian, I could never be entirely sure.

"I don't know what to say. I really am so very sorry." It wasn't hard for me to infuse my voice with genuine emotion, remembering all too well the night Leo was killed. We'd stood in that cold church, my older brother and my sister and I, watching as Leo's small, white coffin came rolling up the aisle, not daring to look at each other or at anybody else. I kept telling myself crying was no use. Leo was dead and no amount of sorrow could undo that fact. "She was so young, so lovely. It really isn't fair."

Vivian laid her hand on my arm. "Will you come to the graveside? It will only be Father, the cousins, and I."

"No Doctor Nichol?" It was a rotten thing to say to her under the circumstances, but I had to know.

She dropped her gaze, fumbling with her purse. "My father doesn't want him there." She raised her head; there were tears sparkling on her lashes. "Will you please come and stand beside me? I would very much appreciate your presence now."

It was an odd request, and I wondered what lay behind it. I wondered, too, why she was putting on the pitiful act. "I wouldn't want to intrude." Not to mention they'd taken out a restraining order against me. Did the funeral mean the cease and desist was temporarily suspended?

"Please." Her smile trembled, almost as if she'd rehearsed the gesture. "It would mean a lot to me."

I had retained the car I'd rented earlier in the week, and I followed the funeral procession to the General Protestant Cemetery on Topsail Road. The cemetery was nestled in a cleft of the Waterford Valley opposite the Southside hills. A place in the Roarke family plot had been set aside for Felice, a hole surrounded by mounds of frozen earth. The weather, clear and bright when we'd left the church, had quickly soured, and ice pellets pummeled us as we huddled around the open grave in the freezing northeasterly wind.

"In the midst of life, we are in death, of whom may we seek for assistance?" The elderly priest's dark vestments flapped and swirled around him, his words all but swallowed up by the howling wind. Vivian slid her hand into the crook of my elbow, her head bent, tears running freely down her cheeks. *It isn't fair.* That's what I'd kept repeating to myself the day Leo was buried. *It isn't fair, it isn't fair.* Nobody expects a life so young to be snuffed out without a warning, without even a good-bye.

A movement at the southern edge of the cemetery caught my eye. Eamonn Molloy stood there, his hands rammed into his coat pockets, his expression grim. He wasn't watching the funeral, though.

He was watching me.

"YOU do remember your family took out a restraining order against me." I handed my hat and coat to the Roarkes' maid and stepped into the front room. "Changed your mind?"

"Perhaps I was overly hasty." Vivian's smile was brittle. "People make mistakes, Mr. Boyle."

"Ah." I wondered whose idea that cease and desist had been.

"Perhaps. Will you have a drink?" Vivian stood in front of the fireplace, warming her hands. The flames reflected carmine and scarlet in her long, dark hair and illuminated her green eyes beautifully. She really was a most handsome woman, and I wondered if the rumors about her multiple marriages were true.

"Sure." I took out my case and offered her a cigarette, lit it for her, and lit one for myself. I was sitting in the same chair I'd had before, and I watched as the smoke from my cigarette was swiftly drawn upward, toward the same invisible seam. I needed to get into that hidden space under the stairs, dammit. I had to find a way. "What have you got?" Poison, probably.

"Wait here." She smiled. "I've asked the cook to prepare something special, just for you."

"You were counting on an awful lot, lady."

I watched her disappear into the kitchen, listening to the clicking of her slippers on the wide board floors. Apart from Vivian and myself, the house was silent, unnaturally still. Mr. Roarke had locked himself in his bedroom as soon as he'd returned home from the cemetery, and the servants, if there were any in attendance, were as quiet as mice. I got up from the chair and, circling behind an overstuffed antique couch, moved to the opposite wall.

The paper was about as ugly as you'd expect and accented here and there with paintings of village scenes, Alpine mountains, and the horrific visages of various Roarke ancestors. I put my face close to the wall and strained my eyes to find a seam, but the light was too poor to see anything at all. I turned each of the pictures and scratched around their backs, also finding nothing; there was nothing under any of the rugs, and the living room furniture—despite its elegant appearance—concealed nothing but dust. My attempt to discover the location of the Roarkes' secret room was foundering badly.

By this time I heard the click of Vivian's heels and settled myself back, pretending to stifle a yawn as she appeared with two steaming cups on a silver tray. "Hot spiced wine." She handed me a cup. "So much more practical in this climate, don't you think?" She sat down across from me, her legs folded demurely underneath her, the cup balanced in one hand. "There's something I don't quite understand, Mr. Boyle." She drew on her cigarette, regarding me through a haze of smoke. "You seemed very moved by Felice's death—in the church and at the graveyard. After all, she was nothing to you, merely an obstacle to your investigation."

So now we were gonna talk turkey. "My brother was killed—accidentally—when I was younger. I guess it's the sort of thing that stays with you."

"How old was he, your brother?"

"He was seven. He got caught in the crossfire in front of a drugstore, back home. It was a mob hit. He... got in the way."

She stubbed out her cigarette and came and sat on the arm of my chair. "I'm so sorry." She leaned close to me, her long hair falling forward and partially obscuring her face. She used her hair like a veil or mask, hiding or revealing herself with merely a tilt of her head. "I forget that you're a stranger here." She touched my cheek with cool, impersonal fingers, a lingering caress.

"Aren't we all?" I smiled at her, and the hand that had been caressing me fell away. "There isn't a single one of us that belongs anywhere, when you get right down to it. It's like the whole thing is some goddamn cosmic joke. I'm sorry." I affected contrition for cursing in front of her. "I beg your pardon."

She lunged toward me, her hair brushing my shoulder, her features blurring into darkness as she kissed me. For a second I grappled with the absurdity of the situation before I managed to return the favor, albeit with much less passion. If kissing Vivian gave me the kind of in I needed, then I'd kiss the stuffing out of her.

"You do that very well." She had somehow ended up in my lap, her hands resting on my shoulders. We were so close I could see the fine lines that fanned out from the corners of her eyes and the even smaller lines that creased her upper lip. "Almost as if you had rehearsed it, Mr. Boyle."

"How the hell do you rehearse a thing like that?" I drew her close to me and kissed her, only this time I imagined it was Sam in my arms instead of some overstimulated dame running on booze and sorrow. I was nearly convincing. She clung to me and began to cry, almost on cue, as if this whole scene was something she'd dreamed up and decided to try on the first chance she got. She started talking—ostensibly to me, but mostly to herself—in a disconnected, rambling fashion. Things about her relationship with Felice, how they'd never really been as close as sisters ought to be, how Felice was fifteen years younger, a late life child and her father's favorite.

"Daddy gave her everything she wanted—the best schools, the best clothes, that car." She got up from my lap and drew hard on a cigarette I hadn't seen her light. "Oh, he bought me a car too. Ordered it from England and everything. Not as nice as the one Felice had."

"You sound a little bitter." I'd seen this movie.

"Oh, wouldn't you? I'm the oldest. I always got short shrift." She stood in front of the fireplace, gazing into the flames. "I was the oldest. Anyway, when things got rough for Daddy, they got rough for all of us."

I went to the sideboard and poured us a couple of real drinks. "What do you mean, they got rough?" I mixed Vivian's drink extra strong. It's an old trick I learned from Charlie, the civilized equivalent of slipping someone a mickey. As far as tricks go, it's no dirtier than most, and I wanted to use whatever I could lay my hands on. Now that Vivian had started talking, it was worth my while to make sure she continued.

"Money," she snapped. "What did you think I meant? Although I suppose you've been doing your homework, haven't you? You probably know more about things than the police do." She took a hefty slug of her drink, and if she noticed it was stronger than usual, she didn't say anything to me about it. "Ever since Mamma died, all anyone can talk about is us. I was in Belbin's Grocery the other day, and Louise Ayre was in there with Dolores Pynn—you don't know who they are, but never mind—and I heard one of them whisper 'double indemnity.' I was never so disgusted in my life. As if something as horrible as my mother's death—" She broke off, her shoulders heaving, and I couldn't help but feel this was yet another carefully scripted performance being enacted for my benefit.

A sudden, subtle noise from the floor above us caused Vivian to turn abruptly, the glass falling from her hand in comically slow motion. Her gaze flickered to the ceiling, then back to me. "You need to go now." Her drink had spilled all over the rug, but she didn't seem to notice or to care. "Right now. Go home."

"Without even a good-bye kiss?" I stood up and went toward her, but she backed away. "That's cold. Maybe you should let me check upstairs for you. Could be a burglar got in while you were away... or it could be a mouse." I started for the stairs, and she practically leapt at me, catching my shoulders and holding on with all her strength.

"Mr. Boyle—Frank—really, I have the absolute worst sort of headache you could imagine."

That old chestnut. "That time of the month?"

She stalked to the closet, pulled out my hat and coat, and all but threw them at me. "You are a disgusting man. Get out, or I'll call the police." She pushed me out the door and slammed it shut. Mrs. Vivian Brooks—nee, Roarke—sure could blow hot and cold.

I stood outside in the yard, marking her progression by the way the lights went on further up the stairs, until a feeble light appeared in the tiny window at the very top of the house.

"Go on up, baby." I watched the house, imagining the scene that was then unfolding behind its staid walls. "Show me where she's hiding."

"NO." THREE weeks later, Sam was fresh out of hospital and clearly feeling his oats; he sat behind his desk at constabulary headquarters like somebody driving a straight six. "Out of the question. Don't even ask." The telephone at his elbow rang. "Lipinski. No. No. I don't care what he says he caught in that net. Those bottles are clearly contraband. Book him." He hung up. "You still here?" It was a cold January day, and any leads I might have had on the Roarke case had blown away on the wind. It seemed everybody in town—the Roarkes, Eamonn Molloy, and Nicky Brooks—were lying low, probably in deference to the weather.

"Uh-huh." I scraped a match off the sole of my shoe and lit a cigarette. "Come on, Sam. One little warrant, that's all I'm asking. I'm sure you're in good with a judge around here. Can't you make it happen?"

"I can't make it happen and I ain't gonna." He swiped at my leg. "Get your feet off my desk."

"Look, I know what I saw." I leaned forward, speaking confidentially. "There's a little room at the top of the house."

"Most people call that the attic." Sam got up and pulled a stack of file folders out of his cabinet. He dumped them on his desk. "You see this? This pile of stuff is all the cases that didn't get solved while I was cooling my heels over at Grace."

"My point exactly. Don't you want to find the woman who shot you?"

"She's in the Roarkes' attic now?" He sat down heavily, and I saw him grimace. He was putting up a good front, but he was far from recovered. What he needed was a week or two of good, solid bed rest, but I knew he wasn't going to get it. Sam hated lying around about as much as I did. The only way I'd get him into bed was if we were both naked. "Look, Frank, I appreciate your difficulties. I agree the Roarkes are hiding something—probably a lot of things—but you can't just go in there and search the house. If anybody goes in there, it's gonna be me, and I'm gonna do it because I suspect there's hidden evidence."

"You suspect something… something to do with Felice's murder."

Sam raised an eyebrow. "Maybe."

"And you've got something planned." I put on my best woebegone expression. "Come on, Sam. Let me in on this. I swear to God, I won't touch anything I'm not supposed to."

"No. The last thing I need's your fingerprints all over a murder weapon."

"Hah!" I thumped Sam's desk so hard he jumped. "So you know there's some piece of evidence hidden in that house."

"Even if I did, I couldn't tell you." He shuffled some papers into a file folder. "Now get lost. I got work."

"So what am I supposed to do?"

"You're a smart boy." Sam winked at me. "I'm sure you'll figure something out."

"Dinner tonight?"

"You cooking?" He rummaged in the desk drawer for a pencil.

"Sure." I stood up and pulled on my overcoat. "Hey, can I ask you something?"

"You can ask me anything." He saw my grin. "Anything that's related to a case."

"If something were to occur on the Roarke property—say, a break-in or property damage—would you have just cause to obtain a warrant? To search the premises, I mean."

"You aren't gonna let this go, are you?"

I shrugged. "I wouldn't be much of an investigator if I did."

He thought for a moment. "Yeah, maybe. If something occurred that was significant enough to justify a search—but you're talking more than just property crimes. It would have to be big. I mean, like murder big."

"So if a body was found on the premises, either in the house or on the grounds, it would pave the way for a search warrant?"

"Yeah, probably."

"Thanks, Sam." I could have kissed him. "You're a genius."

"I know." He grinned. "Speaking of murder, I got the full autopsy report on Felice back from the pathologist." He slid a manila envelope out from underneath the pile on his desk. "Interested?"

"By all means."

"The bullet wound killed her—no surprise there—but a blood sample taken at the time of death revealed significant amounts of narcotic in her body."

That kicked my attention up into high gear. "Dope?" I leaned in to read the report over his shoulder. "So she was drugged?"

He shook his head. "Highly unlikely, since drugs in that quantity would have made it impossible for her to drive. Several witnesses at the scene said they saw her driving down Water Street with a man, remember. She was at the wheel, which means she was habituated to the dope, to the point where it didn't affect her daily functioning." He tossed the report back on the pile. "My guess is, she was addicted, probably getting it from the black market or from a doctor friend of amiable disposition."

"Pretty sure I've got an angle on the doctor friend." People did strange and desperate things when their backs were up against the wall. "So Felice was a drug addict."

"Absolutely." He coughed, took out the inhaler, and sucked back a couple of quick drags. Benzedrine. Were things that bad? I noticed, almost without meaning to, that his hands were shaking. "For what it's worth."

He pushed aside a pile of file folders and something—a slip of paper—fluttered to the floor. I picked it up. It was a letter, written on thin blue airmail paper, both sides of the sheet covered in small, ornate handwriting. "Sam, I think this is yours." The letter bore a Polish stamp.

His expression was unfathomable. He took it, gazing at me as if he expected me to say something. "It's a letter from my uncle. He only just managed to get it out before they...." He pressed his lips together. "Before they closed the whole place up. You know." He traced a gesture in the air. "Sealed it in."

"What?" A cold wind seemed to have sprung up from nowhere. "Sealed it in?"

"The ghetto. My father's youngest brother... he was just a baby when my old man left. I hadn't heard from him for ages, figured he was doing okay, and then last week, bam, out of the blue, I get this letter."

I fingered the delicate paper carefully. "What does it say?"

Sam swallowed hard, scrubbed a hand across his face, and swallowed again. When he finally spoke, his voice was thick with emotion. "It says... ah, he's telling me...."

I laid my hand on his wrist. I didn't care who saw us. "Go on, Sam. I'm listening."

Sam told me that ever since the early days of the Nazi occupation, the Jews of Warsaw had lived in fear. They knew it was only a matter of time before dear old Herr Hitler made his move.

Since 1940, the Nazis had been building a special "Jewish section" or ghetto, and herding people like Sam's uncle into it. Once they got them all inside, the bastards sealed it up. Then they cut food rations, the better to starve the Jews to death. "He was able to get this letter out, but he says he doesn't know when the next one will be. They aren't sure what's going to happen. Some of the neighbors have been... 'relocated.'" His eyes were bleak. "Nothing I can do, right? I'm here and that's happening over there." He pretended some busyness with his desk drawer. "I tried putting a call through to Warsaw, but...." He shook his head.

"Have you told anybody? Maybe someone in North Atlantic Command can help."

"Nope. Tried that. Not in their purview." He laughed, but there was no humor in it. "I guess they got their hands full, bombing the Krauts."

"Yeah, I guess you're right." I couldn't disagree with him. I'd seen the newsreels down at the Paramount Theatre: China's war, five years later; the Nazis in Greece; French children devouring rationed food. There was never anything but the most general information and I understood that, but why was nobody mentioning things like the Jewish ghetto or the suspected forced-labor camps? Both sides had POWs, sure; that was how the game was played and everybody knew it. But why was nothing being said about this?

Sam sighed and folded the letter away. "This whole situation with the Roarkes kind of pales in comparison, doesn't it?"

I wanted to lean in and kiss him, reassure him that something would be done about it, that Yankee might and ingenuity would save the day, but I didn't know if that were true. I contented myself with patting his shoulder. "We'll talk later, huh? In private. I gotta see the doctor."

"Hey, are you sick?" he called after me as I was getting on the elevator. "I don't want to hear tell of you dumping bodies in the Roarkes' front yard. I mean it, Frank. You keep your nose clean or I'm running you in."

It was a cold day, with tiny snowflakes drifting down out of a dove-gray sky. I could have taken a cab, but I knew exactly where I was going and I wanted to walk. I headed downtown, taking the stairs at Garrison Hill maybe two at a time. A bus blared its horn as I darted across the intersection by the cathedral, but I didn't care. I took Cathedral Street at a dead run and skidded to a stop at the bottom.

"Frankie, me boy!" A hand clapped onto my shoulder, and I turned. There was Eamonn Molloy, beautifully turned out in constabulary uniform and looking like the money he'd put on Seabiscuit had come in at twenty to one. "How are you getting on?"

It was like a bucket of cold water dashed in the face. I tried to keep a note of disgust out of my voice, but it was hard. "Very well, and you?" I stepped back out of his reach, and the hand dropped back by his side.

"Haven't seen much of you lately. Spending all your free time with Lieutenant Lipinski?" He looked me up and down. "Like attracts like, as they say."

"It's nice to see you, Chief Molloy, but I'm on my way somewhere. I hope you'll excuse me." I turned away, but he caught my wrist.

"Word in your ear, Frankie." He yanked me toward him so hard I nearly slipped on the frozen ground. "It'd be unwise for you to forge the same sort of friendship with another that you had with me. And I don't need to be telling you that unnatural congress between men is quite illegal."

I yanked my arm away. "You've got a lot of nerve."

He smiled. It wasn't a nice smile. "Have I, now? You know, you should be thinking about the choices you've been making, Frank. This city has the mentality of a small town. People talk. It wouldn't take much to start a groundswell of disapproval, now would it?"

The hair on the back of my neck prickled. "Is that a threat?"

"Not at all." He grinned and clapped me on the shoulder. "Merely a suggestion." He tipped his cap to me. "Be seeing you."

I watched him climb Garrison Hill, taking the wide steps easily, his long body bent forward at the waist, and I wondered what would happen if I ran after him, grabbed him by the nape of the neck, and shoved his face into the icy concrete. Was he actually threatening me? If so, he was a lot dumber than I thought, since he couldn't expose me without exposing himself. The thought was hardly comforting.

Doctor Elmer Nichol's receptionist was a skinny dame about twenty, with a big head and too much sticky red lipstick. She kept me standing at the desk while she paged laboriously through the doctor's big appointment ledger, finding nothing. She sighed heavily, pushed the book away from her, and peered up at me, probably surprised I was still there. "I don't find an appointment for you, Mr. Boyle. I'm sorry."

I took out my wallet and flipped it open so she could see my badge. "Maybe you didn't understand me the first time, sister. I'm not asking for an appointment. If Doctor Nichol is in, I'll see him now, or else I'll come back with three constables and a warrant." The last part was a bluff, but she didn't need to know that. "I'm going through that door into Doctor Nichol's office whether you like it or not. Now you can be a good girl and announce me, or you can sit there like a dumb cluck, but either way, I'm going in."

She swallowed hard and picked up the intercom. I was halfway in the door before she finished. Nichol sat at his desk, his chin in his hands, staring wistfully at a photographic album. "Mr. Boyle, here you are again. I can't help but think you crave my companionship."

"What are you looking at?" From where I stood, I could just make out the figure of a young woman, seated sideways on a chaise with some sort of filmy drape around her shoulders. She seemed to be naked from the waist up, or maybe that was the lighting. "Taking a peek for auld lang syne?"

"Vivian was right." He flipped the page. "You really are a disgusting man."

"As much as I'd love to stay and continue this cozy chat, I'd rather cut to the chase."

He turned a page, moaned quietly, and buried his face in his hands. "Mr. Boyle, I am a man in the throes of sorrow. Can you not, in the name of all that's decent, leave me be?"

"Yeah, I can see how you'd be all torn up." Another photograph of Felice: this time she was nude except for some artfully placed ropes, and kneeling at the foot of a staircase. A second woman, equally naked and bearing a startling resemblance to a younger Lois Temple, knelt in front of her. Both women gazed worshipfully up at the beautiful young man crouching on the stairs above them, his bare torso glistening with oil. He was probably some fisherman's son, poorly educated and eking out a subsistence living in one of the many tiny fishing villages scattered around the island. I could just imagine what the photographer had told him. We had plenty of sharks like that back in good old New York City. "The constabulary's autopsy report on Felice Roarke shows significant amounts of narcotic in her blood. I'm wondering if you might know something about this."

He narrowed his eyes. "Isn't this a bit outside your scope, Boyle? You're an insurance investigator."

"I'm an investigator. Anything that falls within the realm of my investigation, I investigate. By the way, the autopsy report mentions that Felice had previously been pregnant. You know anything about that?" I took the photo album away from him. As I'd suspected, most were pictures of Felice. Some—the majority—were fairly innocent: Felice posed in front of a mirror, one lovely breast bared to the camera, a string of pearls around her throat; Felice lying on her back on a rug, wearing fishnet stockings and a smile; Felice and a second girl embracing in simulated ecstasy. There were some, however, that would have made a hardened libertine blush. "There's no way a girl like Felice, a girl from a decent family, would ever consent to posing for this kind of filth. From what I've seen, she didn't need the money, so I'm thinking maybe she did it for dope. Or maybe you had something on her. Something that'd cause a real big stink if it ever got out."

Nichol shrugged. He simply sat there behind his desk, arms resting on the blotter, gazing at me as if he'd never seen me before. "Are you hoping for a confession?" He laughed. "You really have no idea, Boyle. You're in this up to your neck, but all you can do is flounder around in it like bath water." He stood up and came toward me. "Give me back my book and get out of my office." He yanked the album away from me. "Before I call the police."

"So it was you." I backed away as he came toward me. I could feel the reassuring bulge of the gun under my arm, but there was no way I'd get it out before Nichol clobbered me. I wasn't looking forward to another pummeling at his hands. "You were supplying her with drugs so she'd pose for you. When she started to kick up about it, you popped her. Did you keep the gun? No, you're not the type. It's probably in the harbor, am I right?"

"Nice theory," he sneered, "but this isn't a detective novel, Mr. Boyle."

He swung at me, but I ducked and his huge fist slammed into the door. I twisted the knob and, taking advantage of his momentary confusion, darted into the waiting room, which by now had filled with local people, patients of Dr. Nichol, all of whom peered at me with curious apprehension. He wouldn't dare hit me in front of them, and so I was able to step out onto Duckworth Street, safe—for now—from another beating.

"Why, Mr. Boyle." The voice belonged to the last person I'd expected to see—Lois Temple. Obviously she'd been shopping, her arms were laden with parcels. "How nice to see you again. Grandar is always asking about you." She'd obviously forgotten our acrimonious parting—and the fact that she'd tried to crack my skull with a frying pan. *You, coming up here from New York City, with your fancy suit and your polished shoes, asking questions about things that are none of your goddamned business….*

"Miss Temple." I indicated the parcels. "Perhaps I could be of some assistance?"

"Oh, I don't want to impose." She blushed prettily. "Grandar sent me down to do the shopping and I got carried away. It's so hard to find even the simplest things nowadays."

"I'm on my way uptown. Will you let me treat you to a cab?" I made a mental note to put it on my expense account and hailed the first Crotty's car I saw. When both Lois and I were comfortably ensconced in the back, I said, "That Doctor Nichol sure is a busy guy." There was no frying pan immediately to hand, so the chances she'd clock me were infinitesimal. "You should see that waiting room."

Lois didn't reply, merely rolled her eyes and made a disgusted noise.

"You don't care for Doctor Nichol." I leaned forward, trying to see her face, but she kept it turned from me, ostensibly so she could look out the window.

"I wouldn't sully my mouth with his name." She clutched her parcels, her gloved hands clenching and unclenching.

"He seems to be very highly regarded."

"That's because you don't know him."

We were heading in an easterly direction along Duckworth Street, passing various small shops and cafés. I sat in silence and waited for Lois to speak. I knew if I pushed her too hard, she'd clam up, but if I was patient and gave her time and space, she might tell me something to my benefit.

"Doctor Nichol...." Lois's voice trembled. "He's a destroyer of women." Our cab rounded Cavendish Square, where the Newfoundland Hotel loomed up before us, a colossus. "He gets young girls to trust him, and then he takes advantage."

"What do you mean, Miss Temple?" I touched her arm. Our cab stopped for a red signal. In a few minutes, we would be at Lois's front door and my opportunity would have passed.

"You know what I mean." She turned and stared at me, and I saw her face was white to the lips. "Do you think she's the only one? He makes young women trust him and then...."

"How does he make them trust him?" I had my suspicions, but I wanted to hear her say it.

She darted a glance at me. "He helps them… if they need that kind of help."

"What kind of help, Lois?"

"If a girl's in trouble… he can take care of it." The words tumbled out of her, one on top of the other. "If she has no one to turn to. He can fix things." She wouldn't look at me. "And he doesn't ask for money."

"What does he ask for, Lois? Does he take photographs?" I was careful to speak very softly. "What you tell me could help a lot of other young women."

"I can't." She swallowed a sob. "Mr. Boyle, I'm very sorry." The cab pulled to a stop in front of the Temple residence, and she got out and hurried down the drive.

I SPENT part of the next day in the newspaper morgue at the *Daily News*, not real clear what I was looking for but pretty sure I'd recognize it when I saw it. For a city the size of St. John's, there sure as hell was a lot going on. This place almost rivaled the Bronx for the number and variety of weird events that cropped up. And there were the usual society page features about rich people's weddings, complete with lengthy descriptions of what the bride wore and who'd baked the wedding cake. Most of these were written by someone calling herself merely "Suzi."

One folder held the graduating class photos from Broughton Hall, a private school catering to the young women and girls of wealthy families. I saw that both Felice and Lois were graduates, albeit separated by some five or six years. Interesting how those two seemed to be around every corner. They were hardly contemporaries, yet there they were in Doctor Nichol's private photo album. Maybe he enjoyed debasing the daughters of rich, established families, people whose fathers and grandfathers had exploited the local economy to the degree that their descendants could live comfortably off the proceeds.

Felice I could see—especially if she was pregnant and he was able to help her out. Cue the dramatic music for the sordid little tale: girl in trouble, helpful older man with the right connections makes it easy. St. John's wasn't that big a place, and surely someone knew something.

I pulled a folder of clippings on Elmer Nichol, not expecting to find very much: a faded photograph of the good doctor at his graduation from Dalhousie University, a note about the opening of his practice, and his father's obituary. *Passed away suddenly at his home in the Waterford Valley, Dr. Elias Nichol, aged 58. Safe in the Arms of Jesus.* It was accompanied by a set of photographic negatives, pictures of the funeral cortege, which was comprised of exactly three cars. "Not well liked, dear doctor." Maybe I wasn't the only one who disliked the Nichol family on principle.

Wills were kept by the provincial government, so I hopped a cab up to the Colonial Building on Military Road and spent some time familiarizing myself with the records. Two hours later, I'd failed to find any trace of a will for Dr. Nichol senior. The young woman at the desk advised me that he had died intestate.

People died intestate when they didn't bother making a will; people didn't bother making a will because they either had nothing to leave or they didn't care what happened to what they did have. The administrator of the estate had reported the elder Nichol died without "…such residue as might be expected"—in other words, there was nothing left over. That in itself was pretty damn curious.

Nothing left for Nichol the younger… nothing there for when he emerged from Dalhousie, a newly minted doctor ready to set up a practice of his own. So where had the money come from? He could hardly have rented his premises on Duckworth Street with nothing, and there was the cost of supplies and the payroll for his nurse and the receptionist. Where had the money come from? To whom was young Doctor Nichol indebted?

The Registry of Businesses answered that question, in the form of a snotty young clerk with wire-rimmed glasses and a receding hairline. He wouldn't let me touch the documents myself but insisted on locating the pertinent information as I asked for it. It was like pulling teeth. "As you can see, Mr. Boyle, Mr. Elijah Temple very kindly furnished Dr. Nichol with capital." And there it was in black and white: *...sum of which was paid by Elijah Temple in the amount of $5000.*

It was a helluva lot of money in anybody's book.

"SO WHAT happened to old Dr. Nichol? Surely he made some money from his medical practice. How'd it all disappear?" The end of the workday and I was back in Sam's office, relaxing in his one extra chair and smoking a slow cigarette before I headed home. The early darkness had closed in around us, and the single lamp on Sam's desk cast a circle of warm light.

"From what I gather—and this is public knowledge, so I'm not letting any cats out of their respective bags here—Doctor Nichol the elder gambled rather lavishly on the international markets." Sam leaned back in his chair and loosened the knot of his tie. "When it all went to hell in '29, he lost bad."

"Like a lot of people." I sighed, leaning to snuff out my cigarette, and my gaze lingered on Sam.

"What are you thinking?"

I couldn't stop looking at the soft cushion of his lower lip. "I'm thinking I'd like to kiss you."

"That'd go over real good here." He grinned. "Going home?"

"That was the plan." I reached out and traced the bones of his wrist with my index finger.

"Frankie—" He drew away. "Not here."

"The door's closed." I glanced around. "Hardly anybody ever comes down this hall."

"Sergeant Picco's office is just across the way." Sam indicated the direction with a nod. "Now, how would you like to explain things to him?"

I knew I shouldn't tease him, but I honest-to-God couldn't resist. "Well, it's not like—" I picked up his hand, holding his index finger. "—not like I was doing *this*." I watched his eyes darken as I sucked, drawing his finger into my mouth.

"You're gonna get us arrested!" He yanked his hand away and wiped it on his pants. "And maybe killed and dumped in the harbor—Frankie, I'm not kidding here."

I stood up. "I'm going home." I unhooked my spare key from the ring and laid it down in front of him. "Let yourself in. I'll be waiting."

THE streetcar took me nearly to my door, and it was full dark by the time I got home. I went up, shucked my overcoat, and checked the mail, but there was nothing interesting, only bills. While I waited for Sam, I stripped and took a quick shower, and shaved away the day's accumulation of beard. I slipped into my dressing gown and turned up the heat a little. At a quarter to six, I heard him on the stairs. I pulled open the door before he could get his key in.

"Glad to see me?"

"Uh-huh." I let him in, then closed and locked the door. A couple seconds after that, he had me backed up against it and was kissing me, the heat of his mouth driving everything away except this.

"I see I'm overdressed," he murmured, and so I helped him out with that. I unbuttoned his overcoat and tossed it on a nearby chair. He kicked off his shoes, then bent to peel off his socks, and somehow we left a trail of Sam's clothes from the front door to the bedroom. "Frankie—"

His pale throat drew me like a shimmer of hot metal, and I leaned in to taste him with my lips and tongue, lavishing hot, wet kisses on his skin. I pressed my cheek into the hard muscles of his chest as I slid down his body, teasing the taut peak of a nipple with

159

the very tip of my tongue. He bucked against me, gasping when I mouthed his hard cock through the thin cotton of his shorts.

"Jesus, Frankie, would you just—"

"That's the trouble with policemen," I murmured. "Always in a hurry."

We came together in the middle of my unmade bed, our naked bodies straining against each other, hands stroking and touching in the midst of long, deep, wet kisses. God, I loved looking at him when he was like this: naked and unashamed, completely caught up in the pleasure of the moment, eyes closed and lips swollen from kissing, begging me to give him what he needed.

I settled between his legs, my body pressed against his, both our cocks trapped between our joined bellies. His hand was in my hair, his clenched fingers making a pleasant, singing little pain. I wrapped my arms around him, holding him against me as we moved.

We made love in silence, our bodies meshing and releasing as the sheets grew damp with sweat. I rose and fell, riding an undulating wave of warm pleasure, of peaks and valleys that dragged on me, stopping speech and hearing, softening the breath. And then the valleys disappeared and the peaks rose up and crashed together, and I heard myself groaning, as if from a long ways away. Sam twisted, wrapped his arms around my shoulders, and pulled me down against him. The tips of his fingers dug into my shoulders as he came, panting hard around the climax, his face contorted, silent.

FRED KOESTLER sat behind his big desk at the St. John's branch of Columbia All-Risk, looking distinctly unhappy. Twice he lit cigarettes that he then turned to grind out; he picked up his coffee cup and swirled the contents around. "Boyle, I've spent much of today fielding phone calls. Now, this isn't how I wanted the new year to go."

"I don't know what you mean, Mr. Koestler." I'd been careful to take a seat to the side rather than in front of him. If he couldn't see me, maybe he'd go easier on me. "I've been pursuing this investigation like you asked me to. Is there a problem?" I picked up the snow globe and shook it.

"This investigation into the Roarke matter has dragged on long enough. Really, there's very little we can do at this stage, and I feel that you've wasted too much time. I've had the Roarkes' lawyer on the phone twice already today. He's demanding that we pay up or else."

"Or else what?"

"Or else he's going to file a lawsuit."

"Against me?"

"Against Columbia All-Risk. I don't need to tell you, we aren't interested in that kind of publicity. I've cabled the payout department. They'll be issuing a check."

I waited for him to tell me I was fired. "She's in that house, Mr. Koestler. I know it."

"What you know and what can be proven are two different things, Frank. Now I've given you ample leeway to get this thing tied up. For some reason you've veered off into God knows how many other areas. What's this I hear about you investigating some black marketeer from the States?"

I didn't feel up to explaining about Nicky Brooks or my suspicions about Vivian, so I kept my mouth shut. "Give me more time." I eased myself up out of the chair. "Please. I promise you, she isn't dead. Mrs. Roarke is hidden in that house, and she'll stay that way until long after you've made the payout. This whole thing is an elaborate ploy designed to make us think the woman is dead. It's the oldest trick there is. Fake your own death for the insurance money…. You said yourself the evidence from Signal Hill is inconclusive. Please, give me a chance to tie this thing up properly."

He considered it. "And if you don't find what you're looking for?"

I took out my wallet and slapped it down on his desk. "Then you can have my badge and my credentials."

His eyebrows rose. "You're that sure?"

"I'm that sure."

"All right, Boyle, but on your own head be it. You've got until five o'clock this afternoon to find out if Mrs. Roarke is dead or faking it. After that the payout department will wire the money to Mr. Roarke's bank account." He rapped on the desk with his knuckles to drive home the point. "Five o'clock. Not a moment more."

When I stepped out onto Water Street, the sound of sirens nearly deafened me. I hailed a cab and climbed inside. Mark Donnelly was at the wheel. "What's going on? Did the Germans land or something?"

"You ain't heard?" Mark threw me a glance over his shoulder. "Some big house on Kings Bridge Road is on fire."

As soon as we rounded Cavendish Square, I saw it. Great gouts of black smoke were rising from the Roarke house as beleaguered firemen struggled vainly to contain the flames in spite of the high wind. Mark pulled onto the curb a safe distance away, and I got out. "Can you wait for me?" I asked.

"Sure thing, Frank. I'm just about off duty. But don't get too close to that, huh? That roof looks liable to go at any minute."

He was right. The entire house was engulfed in flames, and the northeasterly section of the roof had been eaten away by the fire and was on the brink of collapse. I found Picco standing with a group of constabulary officers who were busy holding back the crowd, many of whom had gathered to watch the conflagration. "Any idea when the fire started?"

He shook his head. "No. It's been burning for a while, had to be. The house is just about gutted." I saw Vivian standing with her father on the lawn, both of them watching as their home collapsed into a heap of flame and ash, and I really felt sorry for them. If their financial fortunes were as bad as everyone said, this could well be the final blow.

A young constable appeared at Picco's elbow and whispered something in his ear. I saw Picco nod. "They found a woman's body in the house," he said. "In the attic, if you can believe that. She'd been hiding up there in a little room off one of the bedrooms. It—she's pretty badly burned. They're bringing her out now." We stood back as a shrouded body, horribly still and wrapped in sheets, was loaded into the waiting ambulance.

"Thus passes Mrs. Roarke," I murmured. Picco gave me a dirty look, but I ignored him. Columbia All-Risk would have to pay out after all.

An unmarked police car pulled up, and Sam Lipinski got out. "How's it look?"

Picco nodded at him. "Lieutenant. The house is a complete write-off."

Sam looked me over. "What are you doing here?"

"They just brought Mrs. Roarke out." I gestured at the ambulance. "This was no accident. Whoever killed Felice torched this house, you can bet on it."

Picco bristled. "You can't possibly know that. Who do you—"

"Mr. Boyle knows things." Sam squeezed my elbow. "He's got great intuition." His expression said I'd better be sure or it was all our asses on the line. He pulled me aside. "Frankie, now don't kid me on this." He looked tired and haggard, like he'd been running full out for far too long and without any decent rest.

"I can't explain it just yet, but I'm sure." I wanted to touch him, but Picco was watching us, so I kept my hands in my pockets. "Trust me. This was Nicky Brooks."

"Brooks?" Sam grabbed my arm so hard it was painful. "Why? How? What makes you say that?"

"Nicky Brooks came to Newfoundland because the Spinelli brothers ran him off." Something twanged inside me when I said it, the kind of discordant little chime that told me there was more to this than was readily apparent. "There was nowhere else for him to go, and let's face it, the wartime pickings up here are pretty good. He knew where I went when I left New York and he figured he could get his paws on me." I nodded toward the Roarke property. "He probably also killed Felice."

"Nicky didn't kill Felice, Frankie." There was a rumbling groan and a shout went up from the assembled crowd as the roof of the house fell in. Sam took an instinctive step back and so did I. "Felice was shot with a .38—we found it when we searched the house." His gaze slid away from mine. "Since we're talking about Nicky Brooks, I should tell you he's a big part of the reason I came here."

"Oh?" He wouldn't look at me, and I wondered why.

"We suspected the Roarkes were actively involved in the black market, it's true…." Sam shook his head. "But the Roarkes are small fish. Nicky Brooks, on the other hand, he's a big fish."

"Sam, what are you not telling me?" An ugly feeling bloomed, growing inside me like a cancer. "What's this about?"

He gazed past me, his eyes fixed on the burning house. "I told you I was recruited here. That's true. I told you I came up here because things got too hot. That's also true."

Be careful. Watch where you're going and… don't step into any darkened doorways. He'd tried to warn me… that night in my apartment, he'd tried to tell me. "And what else is true? That you were using me as bait?"

"Frank, please. You gotta understand—"

"No, I don't!" He reached for me, but I twisted away from him. "So that's all I was to you? Just a means to an end?"

"No, it wasn't like that." He clutched my sleeve, twisting it in his fingers. "I sent you up here because I thought you'd be safe. I thought if I got you far enough away, Nicky Brooks wouldn't bother looking for you." He relaxed his grip and shoved his hands in his coat pockets. "There wasn't a whole lot of time to pussyfoot around. Brooks was out of Sing Sing. He started asking around the neighborhood: where was Frankie Boyle? He put it around that you and him had business together. He said he'd find you no matter what, even if he had to go to the ends of the earth." Sam grimaced. "Which, for Brooks, is probably Newark, but anyway. I figured if there was gonna be business, better it should take place where I could keep an eye on him."

"You followed him here…. He almost killed me, and you gave him the chance to do it again." One wall of the Roarke house, badly charred, succumbed to the efforts of the firemen, crumbling slowly—almost gently—under the weight of water. "You used me. You gave me a really long leash, and you let me run as far as I liked. All so you could get Nicky Brooks."

"Frankie…."

But he knew it was useless. There wasn't anything to say, not now and probably not ever again. I turned my back on him and walked away. I didn't look back.

Chapter Ten

I WAITED 'til late that same afternoon and spent half an hour in Koestler's office explaining myself. I said I hoped he'd consider keeping me on, but if he didn't, I understood and I left my expense account report with him. Then I lit out for the Heartache Café, a back booth, and a drink. It felt like I'd been on this case for years, moving from one disaster to the next with scarcely a pause for breath in between. I had an uncomfortable feeling this thing wasn't quite over, that I had only scratched the surface of what was a deep and very nasty situation. Felice Roarke was dead, murdered by somebody who sat in the front seat of her car and put a bullet in her brain, and essentially the Roarke family was ruined. Nicky Brooks was still at large and looking for me, thanks to a slimy lawyer with just the right connections to get him out on bail. With any luck at all, he'd find me and put a bullet through my brain but not before he amused himself by beating the hell out of me. Worse, I no longer had Sam to lean on.

"How's the whiskey?" Jack stopped by on his way back to the kitchen, balancing a load of dirty dishes on a tray. "If you don't mind me saying so, you look like you could use a good stiff one."

"A drink?" I tried to smile. "Or are you referring to something else?"

His cheeks flamed, and he looked away for a second. When he turned back, he was grinning. "Just for that I'm going to have Chris inflict his Louisiana special on you. I think they call it swamp water."

I sat back and looked around, in no hurry to get up and leave, having nowhere in particular to go. There were several threads of the Roarke case that could have used tying up, but since Mrs. Roarke had so obligingly gotten herself burned to death, it was probably a moot point. There was nothing for me to do but go home, except I couldn't seem to make myself move.

"Hey!" Chris shot out from behind the bar, his gaze intent on a small, slender man in a camel-hair coat who'd just come in the front door. "You can't bring that in here!"

The man, a lethal-looking revolver in his hand, charged toward the back of the café where I was sitting. "You should have stayed away. You should have minded your own business." He squeezed the trigger and a flurry of shots exploded around me. I dove for cover, overturning an adjacent table and using it as a shield until I got my gun out, but Jack, moving faster than I'd ever seen him, leapt toward my assailant and squeezed off a handful of rapid shots from the automatic in his hand. The gunman jerked backward and cried out as a red stain bloomed on the shoulder of his coat. He charged for the front door and was gone.

Jack's face appeared over the edge of the table. "You okay?"

"Fine." For some reason this exchange was hysterically funny. "Jesus, Jack… is there anything you don't do?"

He holstered the weapon and reached a hand to help me up. "Huh?"

I dusted myself off and checked my clothing for bullet holes. "Café owner, intrepid restaurateur, mixer of dangerous drinks, and crack shot?" I chuckled. "That's quite a résumé."

"Yeah, well, I grew up in Philadelphia. It's a tough town." He stepped over an upended chair and looked around the café. "Lucky he didn't hit anything expensive."

Chris smirked. "You got anything expensive, Jack?"

Jack grinned at him. "Always the wisecracks. Go get your boyfriend on the horn." While Chris was busy on the phone, Jack put on a fresh pot of coffee. Chris returned with more sugar than rations allowed and a pitcher of fresh cream. "Picco's on his way?" Jack asked. He poured a cup for me. It smelled absolutely heavenly.

"He's not at headquarters." Chris sugared his own cup liberally, then tasted it with an effusive sigh. "But they're gonna send somebody pronto."

We drank coffee and waited 'til a ridiculously young sergeant arrived with two constables. "I'm Sergeant Doherty. Somebody shooting off guns in here?"

"You just missed it, Sergeant." I nodded toward the open door. "He went thataway."

The constables Doherty had brought with him fanned out around the café, taking copious notes while the sergeant interrogated me in what he obviously thought was an official manner. "Did he say anything to you before he started shooting?"

I debated whether or not I should toss off a sarcastic reply, but reminded myself the kid was only doing his job. "He said I should have stayed away. I thought he was probably working for Nicky Brooks." I assumed he'd know who Brooks was. It had to be in the files, somewhere.

Doherty peered at me narrowly. "I'm familiar with the recent case involving Mr. Brooks. You and Mr. Brooks are known to each other?"

"I used to work for him when I was a kid."

"Used to work… for Brooks…." He duly noted this down. "This was in New York, I take it?"

"Yes, Sergeant, it was New York."

The phone on the end of the bar buzzed, and Jack went to pick it up. He listened, then held the receiver out to Doherty. "It's Lieutenant Lipinski. He wants to talk to you."

Doherty listened for a minute, then dropped the receiver and was out the front door like a shot. Jack picked up the phone and listened for a minute. "Frank, the lieutenant would like to speak to you. He says it's urgent."

I went cold inside. "I'm sure it is." I nestled the receiver against my ear and leaned against the bar, my back to the room. "Lieutenant."

"Frankie, we got a situation. I figured you ought to know. Nicky Brooks is holed up in an old fishing warehouse on the waterfront, the part the locals call the Outer Battery."

"Uh huh." Was Sam expecting help from me? After what he'd done?

"He's got Picco."

For a moment, I didn't know what he meant, and then it clicked. "A hostage?" Chris was hovering somewhere in the background, wiping tables and setting chairs upright. He didn't seem to be paying attention to the conversation, but you never knew—he and Picco were pretty tight. Hearing that his boyfriend had been abducted by a mobster hell-bent on revenge wasn't likely to brighten his day.

Sam drew a long breath and let it out slowly. "Yeah. Listen, I figured you should know, since you and Brooks are connected."

Yeah. "Connected." That was one word for it. "I'll be there in a minute."

"No, you won't. Stay where you are and keep out of it."

"Your concern is touching," I said dryly. "But I'm coming out there anyway."

"Listen, Frank, the last goddamn thing I need is a civilian getting shot up. Now do as I say and stay put."

I took a cab to the end of Outer Battery Road and followed the flashing police lights to a tumble of ramshackle fishing stores and twine lofts set so close to the water the hungry North Atlantic licked at the clapboards. I identified myself to the constable and ducked under the rope. Sam was standing in front of a large wooden building that had clearly seen better days. "Hello, Sam." It hurt just to say his name.

"Frankie." He clutched my arm like he was asking me for something. "What the hell did I say to you on the phone?" He jerked his head at the twine loft. "He's in there."

"With Picco?" There was no real love lost between us: I thought Picco was snotty and arrogant, and for his part, he regarded me like something he'd stepped in. But that didn't mean I wanted him dead.

"Yeah. Around about six thirty a call came in to headquarters, a man saying he'd barricaded himself in one of these buildings out here. He said he had Picco and was going to shoot him unless we withdrew. You know, the usual thing." He glared at me. "I don't like you being here. I'm gonna get someone to take you home."

"Forget it," I said flatly. "I'll just come right back, and you know it." I sized up the building where Nicky was waiting, wondered which dark window he'd chosen as his hiding place. How the hell had Nicky persuaded Picco to go up there with him? Picco might be a lot of things but he wasn't stupid. From what I'd seen of him, he wasn't likely to walk willingly into an obvious trap. "Been talking to him?"

Sam held up a megaphone. "Brooks? Been trying. Whenever one of us gets close, he starts shooting. He drew a perfect bead on us every time. I don't like it."

"So how do you want to handle this?" I asked. "You want me to go in?"

He looked at me sharply. "Christ, no. You trying to get killed? You stay out here unless…."

"Unless what? I might be the only person Brooks'll listen to, and if it's a chance to get Picco out of there—"

"I said no, Frank. And I meant it."

I stepped close to him, unwilling to air our personal grievances in front of the entire Newfoundland constabulary. "I don't much care what you say, or what you mean. Nicky Brooks and I got history. I'm probably the only one he'll talk to. Without me, you don't stand a snowball's chance in hell of getting Picco back alive. You don't know Nick like I do. He's liable to do anything, just for the hell of it." Christ, he was stubborn. "Let me talk to Nick. I'll tell him I'm coming in. Maybe he'll agree to swap me for Picco."

"I used you." His gaze was bleak. "That's what this is all about." He turned away, his features twisted with pain. "I know I can't ever make that up to you. And I told you not to come out here, but you did anyway."

I knew what he was thinking. "So now I'm here I can maybe do some good?"

Sam beckoned to someone at the very edge of my vision. "Evans, come here."

A burly young constable appeared at Sam's elbow, his breath steaming out into the freezing air, the tip of his nose red from the cold. "Lieutenant?"

"Mr. Boyle here has an idea, and as much as I hate it, I'm inclined to let him try it. Who's your best shooter?"

Evans considered the assembled men before turning back to Sam. "Collins."

"Can you set him up to cover us? Mr. Boyle and I are going in together."

The constable's eyebrows rose. "Mr. Boyle isn't a policeman, Lieutenant." He shoved his hands deeper into his pockets and shivered. "With all due respect, sir, is that wise?"

I shouldered my way into the discussion. "I knew Nick Brooks years ago, back in the Bronx. The reason he came here in the first place is because he's got a score to settle with me." I glanced at the ramshackle building and wondered why Nicky had chosen this place. There was no direct escape route except by sea, and I didn't see a boat moored anywhere nearby. Once the cops went in—and I knew they would, sooner or later—he would be trapped, pinned against a solid wall of rock. "Maybe if we think I'm letting him have me…." I shrugged. "It's worth a shot."

Sam nodded. "If you're right, Brooks'll take the bait."

"I'm sure he will." I felt a cruel satisfaction when he winced. "That was your plan, wasn't it?"

We entered the building with guns drawn, our movements agonizingly slow. I half expected to find an army of Nicky's goons waiting for us, but the place was as empty as a tomb. Sam indicated he would move left, so I took the other side, slipping along the wall.

A shot rang out in the darkness, and I heard Sam curse. "Are you all right?" Too late I remembered what Sam had said about quiet.

"Finally come to get me, Frankie-Boy?" Nicky's voice came from somewhere above me.

"I just want to talk, Nick." A rickety wooden ladder loomed out of the darkness. Was it safe to climb? At this point, did it even matter? "You know, about old times."

"Old times, huh?" A second shot whizzed past me. He was somewhere in the loft, but it was too dark to tell just where. "What old times did you want to discuss? How about the time I killed your kid brother?"

That bastard. He was deliberately needling me, trying to provoke a response. "Whatever suits you, Nicky. I'm not particular about the topic." I fumbled for the ladder and put my foot on it, waiting, hardly daring to breathe. Maybe it was paranoid but I figured Nick could see me wherever I was. "Pretty cold outside, huh? Bet you wish you'd brought your long johns." I stuck my gun in my pocket, grabbed the rung above me, and pulled myself up. The ancient wood creaked and groaned under my weight and I prayed the rickety construction would hold long enough for me to get up to where Nick was. I took a breath and reached for the next rung. "Yeah, they told me it got cold here, but I didn't expect anything like this." The second floor was an open space, constructed so that supplies and materials could be easily conveyed to the lower portion of the building. To the right of me were several piles of rope, haphazardly coiled and shoved against the wall. A stack of crab traps teetered precariously near the edge, in company with a cluster of wooden marker buoys, painted bright orange.

"That's far enough, Frankie."

I squinted, trying to see him, but it was much too dark inside, and the lack of ambient light only served to intensify the gloom. I caught a glimpse of him only when he moved, which wasn't often. Nicky Brooks was taking no chances. There was an open hole cutting through both floors, a disposal chute for offal that let into the ocean. It was maybe four feet across one way and three feet the other, large enough to drop a body through. "Where's Sergeant Picco?" I held tight to the top rung of the ladder with one hand, and eased the gun out of my pocket.

"Oh, he's just fine." Nicky's tone was friendly, conversational. We might have been talking about the weather. "Aren't you?" He kicked the dark bundle at his feet. It didn't move, and made no sound. "He's sleeping it off right now." I couldn't see Picco well enough to determine what Nick had done to him. From my vantage point, he was merely a shapeless presence lying on the floor.

"Did you kill him?"

Nick laughed. "I don't think so, but I can't be sure. These local boys, these cops, they don't stand up to a pistol-whipping like the ones back home." He shoved the bundle with his foot, and it made a feeble groaning noise. "I think he's still alive. Hard to say." He grinned, his teeth a white flash in the darkness. "Maybe it's the change rattling in his pockets, huh?"

"Nick, I want to come up there and talk to you."

"Then lose the artillery."

So he could see me. I leaned into the wall, balancing myself on the ladder, and raised both hands in the air. "I'm gonna put my gun down." I laid my automatic just to the right of the ladder, where he couldn't fail to see it. "It's just you and me, Nick. Just us now." The ocean sighed, licking at the hole in the boards, and the faint sound of other conversation filtered in from outside. "Let the cop go, huh?"

"Don't think so."

"Nick, they're never going to let you out of here. You gotta know that." I climbed up onto the second level and slowly moved toward him. "The place is crawling with cops."

"Maybe I got a way out." He grinned again. "Ever think of that?"

I was scared for him. I knew he couldn't possibly make it. It was like the present and the past collapsed together, and I remembered all the good stuff, how kind he had been to me when I was a kid, how he'd paid for Ma to have a proper funeral. In spite of every horrible thing he'd done to me, I didn't want to see him gunned down. I didn't want him to die. "Maybe I can talk them into making a deal."

"Don't be an idiot." He held an automatic, the barrel leveled at me. He'd shoot me without hesitation. I knew that.

"At least let me check and see if Sergeant Picco is all right?" I started edging toward the forlorn bundle of clothes on the floor.

"Sure, but do it on your knees. Try anything and I'll plug you, but you already know that."

I did as Nick said and knelt on the filthy floor, slowly moving toward Picco. It seemed to take forever, like the whole place had grown enormous and I was creeping across the floor in slow motion. Picco was lying on his side, semiconscious; his face looked like somebody had taken a tire iron to it. Both eyes were swollen shut, and his bottom lip had split wide open, showing the tender flesh beneath the skin. I was pretty sure his nose was broken. A deep cut bisected his forehead, which had swollen grotesquely, bulging over his eyebrows. I bent close to him. "Picco. Can you hear me?"

"Boyle." I wasn't real sure that's what he said. His voice was little more than a tortured whisper. I was amazed he could talk at all.

"He needs medical attention." I turned to Nick, who was watching us with an amused expression. "Let me take him outside, and I swear to you I'll come back in. You can keep me here as long as you like."

Nick laughed. It wasn't a nice sound. "You must think I'm off my rocker, Frankie. Sure I'll let you take him out of here. Then you can send the cops in to shoot me, how about that?"

"Nick, look—"

"I said forget about it! Goddammit, who's holding the gun here?" He released the safety. "So tell me, Frank: should I do you first? Or the cop?" He waved the gun in Picco's direction. "Already had my fun with him, though." He swung his arm so the gun barrel pointed at me again. "Maybe I'll let you have it."

"Nick." Somebody shouted something just outside; it sounded like "Send him in the back" but maybe that was only wishful thinking. "Let me get him to safety. Then you can do whatever you want with me."

He dropped his arm, the gun dangling from his hand. "I'll do whatever I want with you," he said. He drew back and kicked Picco viciously in the ribs. "Him, too."

"Come on out, Brooks." Sam's voice through a bullhorn was surreal and unexpected. "I'll talk to the judge, get him to give you a break."

Nick sighed. "I've had just about enough of this." A few things happened then.

The first thing was, somebody shot part of the shack away with what had to be a tommy gun. Nothing but a chopper can do that much damage to unprotesting wood. The Constabulary had gotten hold of some serious hardware.

The second thing was, Nicky Brooks raised his gun again and sighted along the barrel. It was one of those moments where you think, *Well, this is a stupid way to die.*

And the third thing? The third thing was pretty damn amazing: Alphonsus Picco somehow managed to roll to where I'd dropped my automatic, grab it, and squeeze off three rounds at point-blank range, before Nick even had time to fire. At that distance, he could hardly miss. Nick had just started forward and the first two slugs took him in the chest; the third crashed into his cheek just below his right eye and exited out the back of his head. He opened his mouth to say something but never made it. His expression was one of absolute incredulity, and then he fell facedown on the filthy wooden boards. Nick's mistake—leaving my gun where it fell—was his last.

"Frank, you okay in there?" Sam was yelling through the bullhorn like he was auditioning for a musical comedy. The shack reeked of cordite, and wisps of smoke hung in the air. Picco was lying flat on his back, not moving, and I feared the worst.

"How you doing, Picco?"

He stuck one hand straight up in the air. "Help me up."

"Are you sure? Maybe you shouldn't move." The sound he made was somewhere between a bark and a groan. I reached out and hauled him to his feet.

From outside there came the sound of a great many sirens, fire trucks and ambulances responding to a general call for aid. One of the police cars had been moved closer to the building, and there was sufficient light for me to see Picco and I were standing on a rickety bit of architecture hanging over the open water. The winds were picking up and the waves were booming over the rocks of the Outer Battery. "Maybe we should get out of here before the whole damn thing falls down around our ears." I gave Picco a hand down over the ladder, and then I followed, being real careful about where I put my feet. I reached the bottom and dusted myself off. "Picco?"

He turned his ravaged face to me, so calm and absolutely stoic despite his terrible ordeal, and I suddenly knew what Chris DuBois saw in him. "Yes?"

"Thank you." I wanted to say something else, about how he had a hell of a lot of guts, that he was one of the bravest men I'd ever known, and he'd saved my life, but the words wouldn't come. "You…" I was suddenly close to tears. "Thank you."

Picco went out and down the slope to where Sam and the rest of the Constabulary officers were, but I stood there for a long time, watching that offal hole fill up with dark, brackish water and listening to the moan of the foghorn, somewhere out beyond Chain Rock.

I WAS sitting at my desk about a week later when the phone opened up. "Boyle."

"Frank, there's a call for you from a Mrs. Brooks." Judy, my secretary, had explicit instructions to screen all my calls to within an inch of their lives. "Shall I put her through?"

"Mrs. Brooks? I don't think I know a Mrs. Brooks." I was hoping this protestation would be enough for Judy to curtail the phone call. "What's it in relation to?"

"Hold the wire, will you? I'll check."

I leaned back in my chair while I waited for Judy to come back on the line. It was an altogether horrible day outside, the kind of day made for staying at home with a good book and a pint of Kentucky bonded. I was on the fifth floor of the building, with a view over Water Street and the Narrows—a view frequently obscured by gusting snow and ice pellets. Now and then the wind came roaring around the corner, buffeting the building and making the windows rattle in their frames.

"Frank? Mrs. *Vivian* Brooks—she says you know each other."

"We do." What were the odds? "Thanks, Judy. You can put her through."

A series of clicks, and Vivian Roarke's voice filled my ear. "Mr. Boyle—Frank—I hope you'll forgive me for calling you out of the blue like this. You probably know that Dad and I were burned out of our house. Mother was killed in the fire."

"So you were hiding her in the house." I smiled grimly, even though she couldn't see me. "Hoping I'd what? Give up and forget? Go away and let you get on with it? So when's the funeral?"

"Mr. Boyle, please." She sniffled. "It's been quite a devastating time for us all."

"You have my deepest sympathies." I didn't even sound sarcastic. "If there's any way that Columbia can be of further help, just let me know." *Like a couple hundred thousand dollars' worth of help.* Koestler could say what he wanted, but it was still insurance fraud, and the Roarkes were as guilty as hell. Maybe it was a good thing, the old dear dying the way she did. I wouldn't put it past the Roarke sisters to kill their own mother.

There was a long silence, and I heard her draw a shaking breath. "That's what I'm calling about. You see, I'm afraid I have to ask yet another favor of you, Mr. Boyle. I should be ashamed to ask you, after everything that's happened, but there's really no one else I can turn to." She laughed, a performance as carefully calculated as everything Vivian did.

"Of course, Vivian. Tell me what you need."

"Well, you see, that's just it." Another brave, trilling little laugh. "I'm afraid the matter is highly personal—so personal that I really hate to talk about it in your office."

She was starting to get on my nerves. "I can assure you complete discretion."

"Oh, I know, and it isn't that, really it isn't." She sighed. "Do you think we can meet somewhere?"

"The public library's not too far away," I said. "Or maybe the museum?"

"None of those is private enough." She made a brittle noise that might have been laughter. "I'm sorry. I'm being difficult, aren't I?"

"We could go to the Heartache Café," I said. "I'll buy you a coffee."

There was a long silence on the line. Just when I thought she'd gone, she said, "I try to take a walk every afternoon. Perhaps we could meet somewhere along my usual route?"

My intuition snapped a warning finger against the back of my neck. "Bit of a nasty day for a walk, isn't it?"

"Oh, Frank!" She giggled, and I was glad there were telephone wires between us. I had a sudden urge to slap her. "You'd be amazed how bracing the weather can be. Will you meet me?"

"Where?" When she gave me the location, I just about fell out of my chair. "Signal Hill. I'll be there in five minutes."

"Don't do it." Sam Lipinski stood in the doorway, shaking the snow off his clothes. We hadn't seen or spoken to each other since the showdown with Nick Brooks at the Outer Battery.

"How'd you get in here?"

"I came up the stairs." He took his hat off and held it pinched between two fingers like he always did. "What'd she want?" He explained, "Your secretary said you were on a private call with a Mrs. Vivian Brooks."

"Remind me to fire my secretary." I got up and shrugged into my coat. "As much as I'd love to continue this little chat, Lieutenant, I'm afraid I don't have time."

He caught my arm as I turned to go. It was an annoying habit he had. "Frank, don't go up there."

"Or what?" I buttoned my coat and pulled on my gloves. "You'll arrest me?"

His eyes narrowed. "Goddammit, Frank! We used to be something to each other! What's the matter with you?" He looked tired, like a man who still hadn't gotten over some terrible thing that had happened to him a long time ago. He was pale, and there were dark shadows under his eyes. He'd lost enough weight that his overcoat hung on him in folds.

"You know what happened." My car keys were in the top drawer of my desk. I stuck them into my pocket, turning my back on him. "You used me to get to Nicky Brooks."

"Frank, don't go up to that hill, not to see Vivian." He stood behind me, so close he could have touched me if he'd wanted to. "She's in it with Nicky Brooks right up to her neck."

"What?" I picked my hat off the stand and crammed it onto my head. "That was Felice."

Sam shook his head. "No. Vivian. Strange thing is, she and Brooks hadn't been seeing much of each other for a long time. Word on the street is their divorce wasn't particularly amicable. But when Viv got worried about the family fortunes and decided to do something about it, she tapped good old Nick." He shrugged. "Maybe she thought he owed her."

I started for the door. "You can tell me all about it later. Maybe we can have a couple of beers, talk over old times, huh?" I was trying not to sound cynical and failing.

"Frank!" His voice echoed in the stairwell. "Don't be so goddamn childish!"

I ignored him and went out into the storm.

THE wind had picked up considerably, and I was forced to squint in order to see through the windshield of my car. Navigating Water Street was about as hazardous as picking your way through a minefield in the dark, and I wished Vivian had agreed to a more comfortable meeting place. At the corner of Water Street and the Hill O' Chips my car hit a patch of ice and skidded sideways, nearly knocking over a man with a wheelbarrow full of firewood. Halfway up Signal Hill, I lost traction and began sliding backward. I probably burned up my week's ration of gasoline making it past the first turn.

I parked in front of the tower and walked around the back to where Vivian said we should meet. It was freezing and the snow had turned into a flurry of ice pellets that struck my exposed skin as painfully as buckshot. The wind was strong enough to take a grown man off his feet.

"Mr. Boyle!" Vivian wore a lipstick-red coat with matching hat, and red leather gloves that probably cost as much as I earned in a week. "Over here!" She waved at me gaily, the same way you would if this were a bright July day instead of the depths of winter, and we were both attending a Sunday school picnic. "I'm so glad you could make it. Isn't it just a bracing day?"

"That's one word for it."

"Come look at the view. I swear, on a stormy day, it's like a different world up here." She took hold of my arm and towed me to the edge of the cliff. Through a veil of gusting snow, I could barely make out Fort Amherst, just across the harbor, but everything beyond that was effectively obliterated. "Isn't it something?" Her voice at my ear was low, thrilling—it was probably the same voice she used on Nicky Brooks and every other poor sap she'd conned into marrying her. She was the original *belle dame sans merci* if I'd ever seen one.

"Look, Vivian." I pulled my arm away from her. "This is hardly the best time for an appreciation of the landscape. What do you want?"

She drew back and gazed at me, a faint smile playing about her lips. "Why, to tell you the truth. Isn't that what you deserve?"

"I'm listening."

"Where should I start? Oh, come over here, in the shelter of the tower. You look half frozen, you poor thing."

It wasn't a position I'd have chosen. With my back to the cliff, I was easy prey for whatever she had in mind, but turning around would have meant standing into the wind, and I was cold enough already. "Get on with it. I haven't got all day."

But she took her own sweet time, Vivian did, pulling out her cigarette case and extracting one, then looking around with feigned helplessness for someone to light it. I held the match cupped in my hand, guarding it against the wind. She took a deep drag and exhaled, the smoke rushing upward with the wind, then falling away. "It was me, you know. Your policeman friend was right."

"Felice?"

"Mm." She exhaled more smoke. "And him." She slanted her eyes at me. "That night he took you to supper at the Heartache Café. I waited for him, and when he left, I followed him home."

"You shot Sam. You shot a cop." I clenched my fists. I'd never hit a woman before, but I was willing to make an exception. "You goddamn bitch." And she put a bullet through her younger sister's forehead, in broad daylight. Christ.

She threw back her head and laughed. "Oh, Frank. So dramatic." Her hand brushed my cheek, and I slapped it away. "The two of you got nosy. Nick and I had a good thing going here. My God, Frank, my father lost everything! What the hell was I supposed to do?"

"I dunno, Vivian. Get a job, maybe?" I moved away, into the teeth of the wind. Just being near her was making me sick.

"He said you'd be angry." She smirked. "He was right."

"Nicky Brooks?" My heart pounded so hard I could feel it in my back.

"Eamonn. He didn't know anybody when he first came here, so we decided it would be nice to make him feel welcome, Father and I. We became quite good friends, the three of us. Eamonn is a very understanding man. He knows what it's like to be suddenly poor." She drew on her cigarette, then tossed it away. "I intended to introduce you to each other, but I see you managed that quite nicely on your own. And he was just the thing to keep you busy." Her smirk made me feel sick. "Did you enjoy him?"

I said something uncomplimentary to a lady and started walking away. If all she wanted was a father confessor, she could find somebody else. This conversation didn't exactly constitute a signed affidavit, or a confession of guilt. Telling me this, now, without a single witness meant nothing except that she'd brought me here to gloat. Vivian was the clever sister, the one who planned everything down to the smallest detail, who always knew exactly how many cards were on the table. Felice didn't have the brains to run a lemonade stand, never mind a black market operation on the serious q.t. I'd had the whole thing figured wrong from the start, except Mrs. Roarke really was dead now, and there was nothing anybody could do about it. Of course she was hidden in the house, and of course the Roarkes had faked her death—but there was no satisfaction in any of it. Eamonn Molloy was bent, Picco was a genius, and Sam and I were through. I stood at the edge of a cliff in a blinding snowstorm, with nothing underneath me except two thousand miles of North Atlantic Ocean. Maybe turning my back on her wasn't the smartest move I'd ever made. I just wanted to get away from her. The dame was rotten, through and through.

"Quite a view, isn't it?" It could have been her finger digging into the middle of my back, except it wasn't. The roaring wind meant I hadn't heard her approach. I understood why she'd chosen the hill as our rendezvous point.

"Is that the gun you killed Felice with?"

She pushed, and I took an inadvertent step forward. A couple more of those, and I'd be fish bait. "All you had to do, Frank, was tell that nice Mr. Koestler that my mother was dead. That's all." She cocked the hammer. "But you couldn't leave well enough alone, could you?" A couple more shoves, just for good measure.

"Listen, is there some reason you brought me up here? Or did you just want to have a little talk and see me grab some air?" The wind was whipping the tails of my coat and driving ice pellets into my face. I was at the very edge of the cliff now, looking down into the foaming, frothing sea. The way I figured it, I could get it one of two ways: either she'd shoot me in the back, or shove me over the cliff. There was no third way about it.

They say right before you die, your whole life flashes before your eyes, but not me. All I saw was Sam.

Sam's a police officer. He just made detective, didn't you, Sam? Back there in New York, standing in Dutch Lipinski's butcher shop among the roast chickens and pails of ground beef and hanging sausages—was that when I knew I loved him? Or was it when we were sitting in his kitchen, eating the good meal he'd cooked himself and listening to the radio? What about the night he'd driven me home after I was let out of the lockup, and stayed to make love? Or the day I saw him collecting evidence of Felice's murder? Was that when I first loved him? It was none of these times and none of these things.

"You'll probably get away with it." I spoke over my shoulder. "Seeing as how I'm liable to get chewed to bits down there. That ought to make you happy. It's the perfect crime."

"I'll make sure to cry when they bring your body ashore." She laughed, and I swear I heard something of Nicky Brooks in it. I couldn't look at her. I turned my face into the wind and waited.

"Go on," I said. "If you're going to do it, then do it."

A hand closed on my shoulder. So she was going to push me over. Good thing I wasn't afraid of heights. "Kinda wonder why you bothered bringing the gun."

A gust of freezing wind ripped open the front of my overcoat, and I was bathed in a sudden, dangerous chill. It was easily four or five hundred feet down, which meant I'd hit the water before my brain had time to register the drop. There would be a sudden shock, and if my heart didn't stop right then, it would take maybe five minutes for my core temperature to drop so low I couldn't be revived.

I was going to die, and it wasn't scary or even funny—it just *was*. The hand on my shoulder tightened. "So get it over with already!"

"Easy now, Frankie. I got you." Sam. It was Sam. All my breath went out of me at once, and I swayed, teetering on the edge of that awful cliff. "I got you." He pulled me around to face him and walked us both away from that terrible abyss. "I got you." I risked a glance behind me. Constable Doherty was handcuffing a fuming Vivian Roarke while another constable secured the scene.

"How'd you know?" My mouth was as dry as the Sahara, and it came out like a tortured croak.

"I've known you all my life, Frank. I knew you wouldn't be able to resist coming up here, even though you knew she'd probably try something." He squinted into the wind and tightened his grip on my arm. "I followed you." He grinned. "I got you."

A moment's hesitation—an eye blink or the beat of a heart—and I flung myself into his arms, holding on as if my life depended on it. I'd be damned if I'd ever let him go again. "Yeah, you got me, Sam." Even the icy January winds couldn't put out this flame. "You had me all along."

EXPENSE Account: Frank X. Boyle

> Submitted to: Columbia All-Risk Insurance, Newfoundland branch

> Carfare, Newfoundland Street Railway: $2.50

> Medical care for scratches inflicted by Vivian Roarke's fingernails: $14.75

> Drycleaning of various items of personal wardrobe: $4.30

> One bottle of red French wine, imported from New York: $7.75

REMARKS: I stand by my theory that Mrs. Roarke had been hidden in the house by her family, who intended to present a fake insurance claim. Vivian Roarke, knowing her mother was very much alive, sought to deflect my investigation by means many and various, the last of which very nearly killed me. It just goes to prove what I've always suspected: the female really is deadlier than the male. Mrs. Roarke was hiding in a secret attic room, the same secret attic room built by the Roarkes' relative after the Great War, to hide his deformity from the world. She was killed in the fire that destroyed the Roarke house; the police identified her by a serial number incised on her dentures, which she'd had made by a famous prosthodontist in New York. It really was exactly like I'd figured it in the first place, only with a whole lot of static in between.

The results of my investigation? Mrs. Roarke's death was accidental—albeit, somewhat delayed—and the death benefit is absolutely payable to the Roarke family.

Yours truly, Frank X. Boyle

SO NICKY BROOKS is dead, and by anybody's reckoning, that should make me free—except I can't stop my mind from turning the whole thing over and over, trying to make it come out right. The scheme Nick had with Vivian, the distribution of black-market goods, makes perfect sense when you consider the state of the Roarke family finances. Sam admitted he'd used me as bait to bring Nicky to Newfoundland, but it occurred to me that Nick would have probably come after me no matter what. I ran this hypothesis past Sam early one Saturday morning, while we sat in the Heartache eating one of Jack's excellent breakfasts.

"I know you can't tell me anything definite, this being official police business and all...." I paused to drain the last of my coffee, signaling Chris for a refill. "Nicky Brooks and Vivian—they were dividing up the black market between them, weren't they? Did Vivian plant that gun in my apartment?"

Sam pushed away the detritus of his breakfast, sat back, and lit a cigarette. "Frankie, it's like this: Nicky Brooks got sent up for killing your brother, but believe me when I tell you, there were dozens of unsolved cases on the books—bootlegging, illegal gambling rackets, pornography, and prostitution—all of them leading back to Brooks or some member of his syndicate. I knew Brooks said he was coming after you when he got out, and I also knew it would be real easy for him to disappear—at least, it would be if he stayed in New York."

"We've been over this already. You figured you'd use me as bait to lure him up here."

Sam made as if to say something, sighed, and thought better of it, and a lengthy silence descended between us. "Yeah, but not exactly." He glanced up as Chris appeared with the coffee pot and waited 'til he'd refilled our cups and gone. "Mostly I was using me. See, you probably don't remember, but it was my precinct that ran him in the first time. I was pretty new to the force, just out of high school, but I knew Nicky Brooks was as big a fish as we were liable to catch on any given day."

"But you couldn't keep him locked up forever."

"We couldn't. At best he'd get manslaughter, and some *schmendrick* lawyer would make sure to plea bargain it down as far as possible." He shrugged. "Nicky gets out, he knows we're still gunning for him, and he disappears. Unless…." He tossed his napkin onto the table. "Unless we get him someplace he can't disappear. Some place where there's more open spaces and a lot fewer rat holes for a guy like him to hide."

"But what about the other stuff?" I lit a smoke and leaned back in my chair. The sun had just cracked the top of the Southside Hills and was lighting fire on the harbor. "The problems you were having at the precinct, the intimidation and threats—just a con job?"

Sam shook his head. "No, that was real. I can still feel their boots in my ribs." For a fleeting second, the memory of that time shadowed his face and hollowed out the spaces under his cheeks, and I wanted to reach across the table and pull him into my arms. "All that stuff that went on at the precinct was just icing on the cake. Sometimes, things just work out."

"You lured him here, where you could get him out in the open. Being the kind of guy he is, he thinks he's hit the jackpot." I took a sip of my coffee. "He gets me, he gets you, he gets a nice little slice of the local black-market pie."

Sam rolled the tip of his cigarette around in the ashtray, dislodging some of the ash. "They found his body, you know." His gaze flicked up to mine. "They pulled him out of the water, down by the American docks." He took his time asking the next question. "He was real special to you, wasn't he… once, I mean." His expression, when he looked up at me, was pained.

"Once."

"And what about Chief Molloy?"

This time I did reach out. I closed my hand around his wrist, squeezing gently. "Chief Molloy is nothing to me. Absolutely nothing."

"You know he planted that gun in your apartment. He was in real deep with the Roarkes." He laughed. "I'm gonna enjoy testifying against him at his trial. You sure you're not still hung up on him?"

I grinned, releasing his wrist. "I'm sure."

"It's a beautiful Saturday," Sam said. "Anything you want to do?" I leaned across the table and told him. To his credit, he actually blushed. I didn't think men did that any more. "That's what you want to do?" He raised his eyebrows. "All day?"

"All day." I took out my wallet and tossed some bills on the table. "Are you up for it, Lieutenant?"

"Oh, absolutely." He held the door open for me as we left. "Lead on, Mr. Boyle." He caught hold of my elbow and squeezed gently. "Lead on."

J.S. Cook was born and raised on the island of Newfoundland. She holds a BA and an MA in English Language and Literature and a BEd in post-secondary education. She makes her home in St. John's, Newfoundland, with her husband Paul and their two spoiled rotten dog-children, Lola and Sheppie.

J.S. Cook also writes as JoAnne Soper-Cook.

Facebook: https://www.facebook.com/AuthorJSCook
Twitter: https://twitter.com/jsopercook
LiveJournal: joannesopercook.livejournal.com
Website: joannesopercook.net

Also from J.S. Cook

http://www.dreamspinnerpress.com

Also from J.S. Cook

http://www.dreamspinnerpress.com

Also from J.S. Cook

http://www.dreamspinnerpress.com

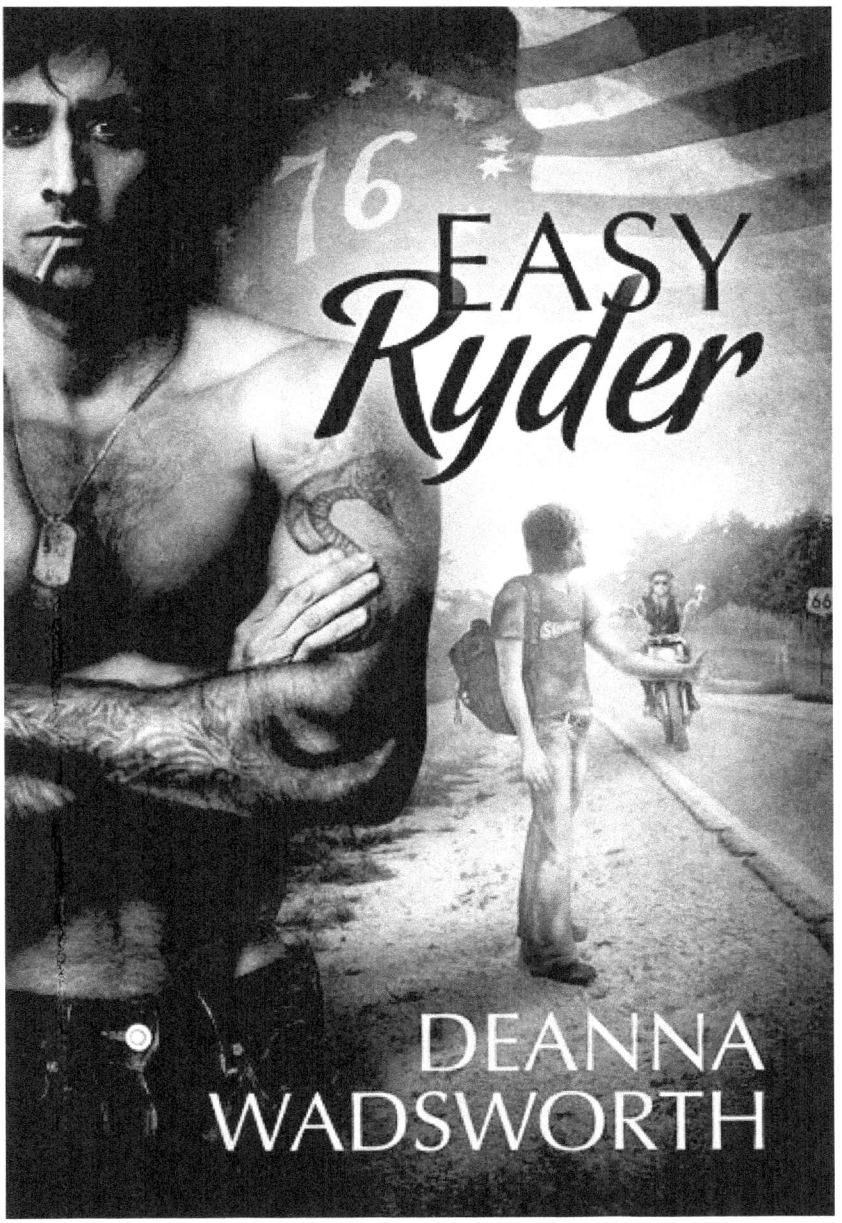

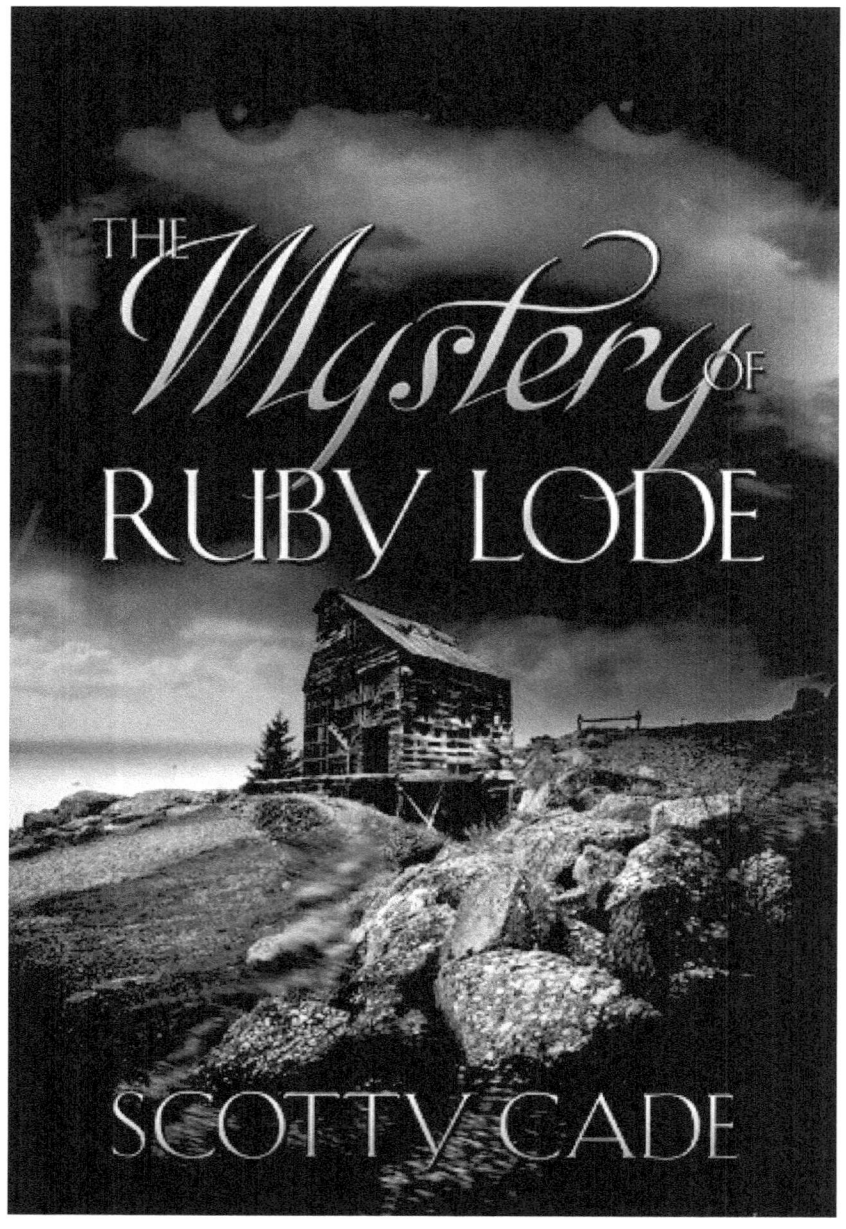

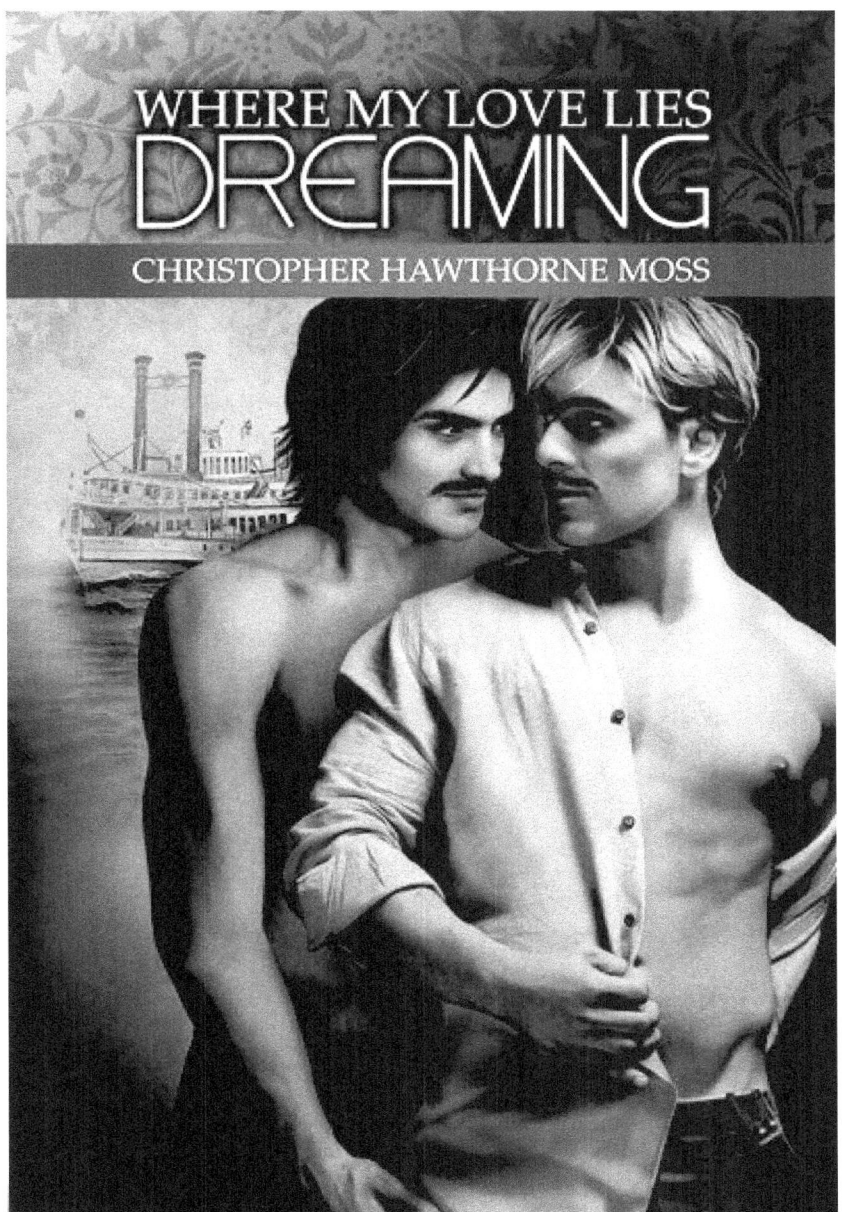

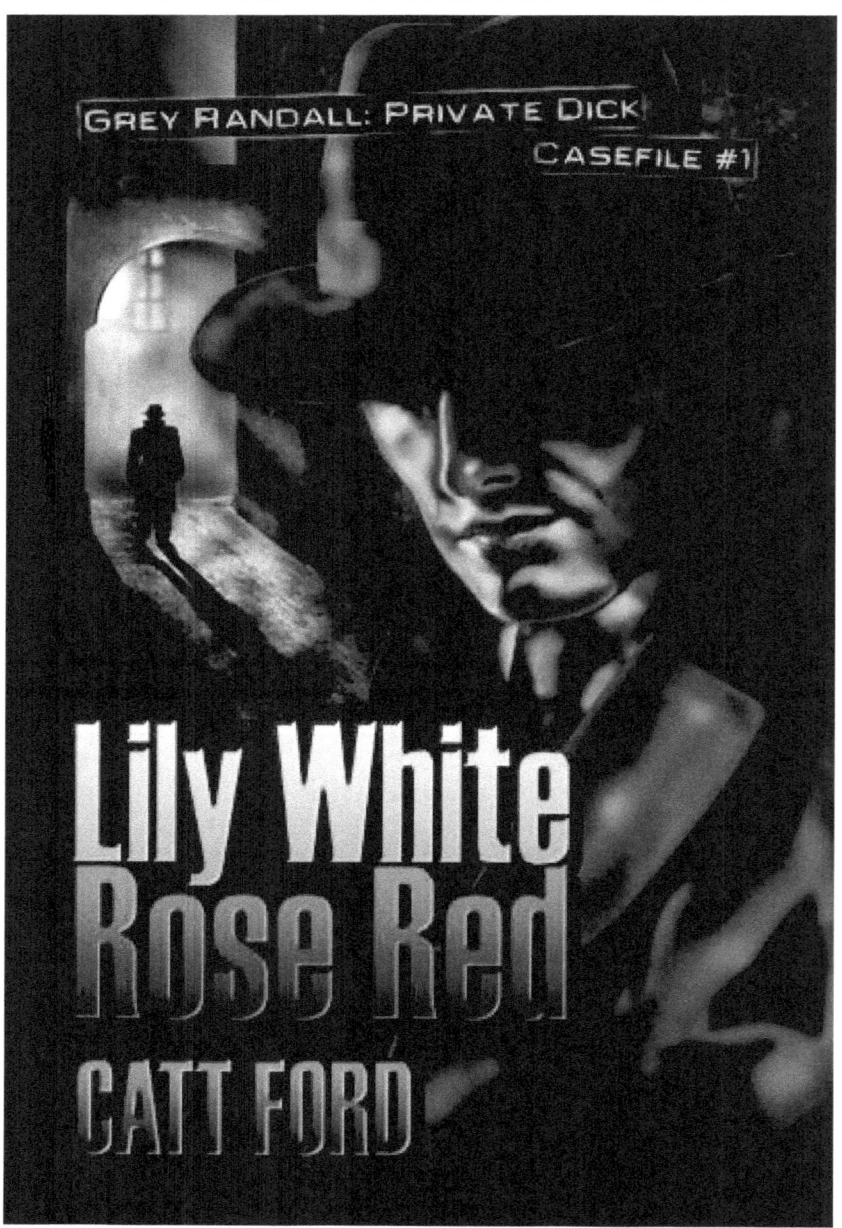

www.ingramcontent.com/pod-product-compliance
Lightning Source LLC
Chambersburg PA
CBHW060056260626
47160CB00005B/1686